Three Star with a touch of Caviar

Caroline Briault

Three star with a touch of Caviar

DEDICATION

This book is dedicated to my wonderful Mum, Brother and husband my fantastic friends, and the lovable 'Uncle' Ray Norman who left this world far too soon.

CONTENTS

Three star with a touch of Caviar

Three star with a touch of Caviar

ACKNOWLEDGMENTS

I must start by thanking all the wonderful people who have supported me in the development of this book from my cover to proof-reading. I honestly could not have done this without you.

Three star with a touch of Caviar

CHAPTER 1

Jessica looked out of her cottage window, watching the rain lash down over her beautifully manicured front garden. Adjusting her silk dressing gown and running her fingers through her newly coiffured hair, she took another sip of her black coffee and watched Frank Small, the elderly local postman, struggle towards her door reassembling a heavily laden drowned rat. Jessica opened the window "It's raining out here Mrs Crewe, I am gasping for a cuppa and rest, what with my heart problem, and my war wound fighting for this country". Jessica looked down her nose, observed Frank and cringed at the thought of him entering her pristine cottage. She held her hand out of the window, hoping no contact would be made with his old wrinkled skin when taking the small bundle of post. "Thank you, Frank," she said and closed the window, watching him limp his way back up the path. "I bet he puts that limp on for sympathy, just like that housekeeper of mine" thought Jessica, watching Frank struggle with the front garden gate.

At one time Jessica had a little more sympathy and patience for others but over the years she realised being nice got you nowhere; the only way forward was to be thin and have nice nails. Jessica certainly didn't care for Frank Small, war hero, postman or not - or his common wife Agnes, who was the local village psychic. Indeed, Jessica had once called upon the psychic services of Agnes to determine if the spirits would guide her to discover if she would have a baby brother or sister. Agnes had plonked her large frame on Jessica's chesterfield sofa and drunk what felt to Jessica to be a gallon of tea out of Jessica's prized bone china cup. She also ate her body weight in biscuits that Jessica had only put on the table as display. Jessica, who had not eaten a biscuit in a long time, watched as Agnes crammed her expensive handmade Harrods crumbly delights into her large mouth, noisily chewing and spraying crumbs onto her Persian rug, whilst falling in and out of a trance, assisted by her spirit guide Dave. The trances caused Agnes to roll her eyes back, gasp and claim a large man was entering her from behind. Her whole body shook for five minutes and she then revealed to Jessica she would have a baby sister. Jessica, although happy to hear about her soon to be sibling, then tried to rush Agnes out of her cottage, fearing that one of Agnes's fits would damage one of her Royal Doulton figurines or leave a trail of crumbs in her wake. Jessica finally managed to escort Agnes to the front door, placing fifty pounds into her sweaty palm and managed to wave the mystic away. Instructions had been given to Mrs May, Jessica's housekeeper, to clean the cottage from top to bottom and get rid of the smell of 'Tramp' - it appeared that Agnes still loved the 80s classic perfume. Just like Agnes, thought Jessica, delightfully tacky with a hell of a lot of front. Jessica also later found out that she was in fact having a baby brother and vowed that's what happens when you trust common people.

Mrs May always arrives at 09:00 every morning and always meets with Frank at the gate for a gossip. Today she was helping Frank out of the gate "I bet they compare limps, pair of malingerers" Jessica thought. Mrs May was a full-figured lady who, although large, did not appear to be fat. She had reached the grand age of 51, the long-suffering housekeeper of Jessica Crewe. Her limp had developed after a freak accident in her early 20s whilst competing in the World's Strongest Woman competition. Mrs May still remembered the painful day whilst on stage, posing with her oiled muscles bulging in a pink bikini, when she slipped in a pool of baby oil and flew forward off the stage into the terrified crowd. Mrs May, then known as Hurricane May, hurtled ahead, arms splayed forward, landing with her legs straddling around poor old Mr Ricket - who it was rumoured was having a sneaky five knuckle shuffle under his paper throughout the competition. Mrs May's leg never recovered from this incident and Mr Ricket was pronounced dead at the scene, although it was reported that he had a big old smile on his face! The last few years Mrs May threw herself into the role of housekeeper, only venturing out of her hermit life after the publicity of the fateful event had passed.

Jessica's eye fell upon the handwritten letter on the top of the pile, she ripped the letter open and exclaimed "oh my!", after reading the letter twice. The letter was informing her, courtesy of Rollock solicitors, that her Aunt Mabel had passed away in what appeared to be mysterious circumstances and had left Jessica her three-star hotel in Zante Greece. Jessica had not had contact with Aunt Mabel since a family dispute between her brother - Jessica's Daddy – and herself. Jessica had fond memories of Mabel, who stood up to Daddy, strongly believing in the power of women. Mabel had not married, much to the disgust of Daddy, who believed that all women should marry by the age of twenty-three, as that was a good breeding age for women. Mabel was rumoured to be somewhat of a live wire. Daddy had insisted that he simply could not associate with his sister, due to her voting labour, running businesses and reading The Female Eunuch in her younger years.

Daddy had, in a fit of rage, tried to marry Mabel off to one of his university chums to tame her. His friend, according to Mabel, was an ageing simpleton, who still lived with his mother and looked like a less orange Donald Trump. Mabel refused to be sold to the fat, spoiled tantrum-throwing Trump-alike and stormed the most popular of Daddy's gentleman's clubs one fateful night, much to the shock of Daddy, who was enjoying a glass of port with his golfing chum, Dr Prevo. Daddy and Prevo both shared very strong views about woman and Prevo had a dislike for the female kind. Daddy suspected that Prevo was perhaps what he called a whoopsie, due to his admiration of the young male form. Prevo believed woman should be seen and not heard and was extremely put out when Mabel stormed the gentleman's club with a number of likeminded feminists. In one swoop they removed their bras from under their shirts and burned them in front of an all-male misogynistic audience. Mabel shouting loudly that she was a feminist and proud and would not be married to Trumpton. Daddy stood up, waving his port, and shouted "They should never have been given the vote!" The misogynists took cover under the tables as the feminists launched themselves at the men, vowing to hang them up by their dangly bits. Prevo tutted and looked a little green, as a big breasted feminist waved her naked chest in his face. Daddy and Mabel squared up to each other as the room fell silent. "Now Mabel, go home like a good girl. Bally well sort yourself out, leave and take your woman's problems with you" Mabel, in one swift move, launched herself at Daddy, landing a heavy punch on his nose. The feminists followed suit, throwing themselves at the remaining men. Daddy, who had been a Field Marshall in the Korean war, jumped away, pointing his umbrella at her. Mabel had then laughed at Daddy's stricken face and left the club with the feminists all astride their Harley Davidson's, speeding away, kicking up dust and flipping the bird to the scared looking customers of the gentleman's club.

Jessica had suffered years of loneliness stemming from being sent to boarding school at the age of five, after being cared for solely by nannies. She rarely saw her parents, who made it obvious that Jessica being female had been a huge disappointment, as the family name would be scuppered. Daddy made his views clear about women and had despised Mummy for not being a good breeder; his mantra being "Woman breed, keep things tidy and look nice for their men, that's just how it is". Mummy seemed content hosting dinner parties and running the large country house, ensuring all of Daddy's needs were catered for; turning a blind eye to all of his mistresses, until her head was turned by Ahmed. He had rescued her one day, when the Merc broke down - he had repaired the car, and her heart, and from then on their romance blossomed. After that day, Mummy had made a point of going into the unknown world of the corner shop to buy milk, even though the local dairy brought an order to the house every day. Daddy was oblivious to their affair until, one morning, Mummy didn't bring him his Telegraph. This was highly irregular, as that was one of her duties - to deliver the paper to him at exactly eight o'clock in the morning. He had heaved himself out of bed, opened the bedroom door and shouted "What's going on?" along an empty hall. He had spent the whole morning waiting for his breakfast and paper, getting more and more annoyed. Eventually he wandered along the hall and down to the women's room (also known as the kitchen to him), determined to tell her this just wasn't how things were done and if she was having women's issues, to bally well get over it.

The kitchen was empty. Something was clearly a foot, he thought, as his stomach rumbled. He phoned his chum, Dickie, who asked his wife Mary to sort the matter out. Mary arrived, rolling up her sleeves and checked Doreen's bedroom in the hope she wasn't ill. She found a note on the bed, addressed to Daddy, stating that she no longer wished to be treated as a housekeeper and she had found love with Ahmed and was starting a new life running the corner shop. Daddy was dismayed! "An Arab! Corner shop? Who will look nice and look after the house? That's what women do!" Daddy had flown into a rage when he realised that his bed was not made, he was hungry, and he didn't have his paper. Mary recommended employing a housekeeper, although Daddy had scoffed when he realised he would have to pay a woman for doing what women clearly enjoyed - keeping things nice. That's it I need a bally wife immediately, he thought and started ticking off his various mistresses and scoring potential villagers out of ten.

Jessica had made one friend whilst at boarding school, but the relationship soon faded after Daddy forbade her to be friends with a girl with short hair, who wanted to have a career in the army "I don't want you getting those funny ideas, woman don't join the army or have short hair. That's just the way it is". Aunt Mabel had fought Daddy on this point, exasperated by his views, but however much Mabel tried to ensure Jessica didn't turn into a glorified housekeeper for a rich moronic man, Jessica was strongly encouraged to marry and be a good wife after leaving finishing school. Much to Mabel's disgust, Jessica had married Justin in a lavish wedding, but Daddy was pleased that she was married off and thought, although Justin had some funny ideas such as washing –up and hoovering himself! Daddy didn't understand why any man would want to do housework and initially became suspicious of him. Over time, however, Daddy began to realise that if Jessica didn't marry him there might be a possibility, she may get too old to marry and end up staying at their large country manor house forevermore. This would be inconvenient as, although the country pad was large, it only had one television and Daddy didn't want to be disturbed whilst watching the horse racing or the news. With that in mind Daddy decided to welcome Justin into the family fold.

For Jessica, meeting Penny at her local yoga morning group had been a huge relief. Justin was flying to and from Tokyo for important business meetings and, apart from the odd letter from Aunt Mabel, she felt quite alone. Penny lay her yoga mat next to her and Jessica was impressed with how confident and sophisticated she appeared to be. Penny was extremely well groomed, rail thin with long dark shiny hair and perfect make-up. Penny was exactly who Jessica wanted to be. Initially Penny made Jessica feel she could depend on her. As their friendship grew, Penny gave Jessica the confidence to have her blond hair styled in the best salon and showed her how to apply her make-up properly. Jessica had turned into the one thing Aunt Mabel would have hated - a snob. After five months, the friendship changed and Jessica noticed Penny had an edge to her. They still shared their love of champagne, fashion, the latest diet fads and Botox but their relationship turned from firm friends to competitive enemies. Their love and hate relationship knew no bounds, ripping apart the appearance of others and each other. But however, much Penny sniped at her,

Jessica did not want to be lonely and friendless again. She grasped onto the friendship with all her might as a lifeline, pleasing Penny and funding their exclusive lifestyle. Justin was not keen on Penny, he believed there was something very dark about her. He had met her twice and both times he had got the feeling something wasn't right about her at all. Penny was supposedly married to a wealthy man called Burt. In the village, however, there were numerous rumours about Burt – the most repeated one suggested he had been in prison for exposure. Penny refused to talk about him, and they were never seen together. Equally Jessica was never invited to their cottage and seemed, in the most part to, be taking over their home. Penny also didn't talk about her past and would change the subject whenever she was asked about her life before meeting Burt. No matter how much Justin tried to warn Jessica that Penny wasn't all she appeared, the more defensive Jessica became.

Jessica phoned Daddy, who was absolutely disgusted that Mabel had left her the hotel and believed she had died and left the inheritance in her will to Jessica just to spite *him*. "Women don't do business, that's just the way it is! Look what happened to Mummy! She got ideas above her station and now is working and breeding with an Arab in a flat above a corner shop, it's just not right". Jessica had become a lot closer to Mummy since she was living with Ahmed, who treated her like a princess, and she had thrived working in the little shop. She had also given birth to another child, her stepbrother Mounir, and they seemed a very happy family unit. Mummy had turned her life around in the fourteen years since she left Daddy, although she was still constantly surprised that people walked to a shop and didn't just order from Harrods. She had turned into the bargain queen and enjoyed going to shops like Asda and Lidl. She had even started shopping for clothes on the high street and was a huge fan of 'Primani'. Although Jessica loved how happy her mother was, she kept it a secret from Penny, who would never have walked into a corner shop or purchased high street fashion. Penny's snobbery would not cope with the likes of Mummy.

Daddy found he was unable to cope in the large house and was constantly surprised by the way it seemed to get untidier by the day. He tried to move in a few mistresses who, unfortunately, did not "cut the mustard" according to Daddy, who had a very strict criteria when it came to choosing women. The final straw for Daddy was when he held a dinner party to introduce his latest potential bride to his golfing chums. He had met Sarah at Sandown horse racing track and was amazed to find that she didn't just go to the races to admire the pretty horses! She could read form! Daddy found this highly useful and believed that he would be able to send her out to the betting shop with ease, maybe even increasing his profits. She was also twenty-six, breed-able and quite nice to look at from the right angle. Daddy had proposed to Sarah within a week of meeting and Sarah had moved into the Manor house. Things started to deteriorate when, on the first day of living together, Sarah asked where the housekeeper and cook were. Daddy had explained that when people get married, that's what women do. Sarah did not seem to agree and refused to deliver his paper to him in the morning and told Daddy to make his own breakfast at the weekends, as she wanted a lie in and Sundays off. Daddy was desperately regretting the proposal but had already arranged the dinner party. Sarah had, only that morning, sat in the lounge reading the Guardian and refused to burn it in the open fire, however much Daddy had stamped his feet. Daddy spent the whole day dreading the arrival of his friends for the dinner party and was even angrier that Sarah had hired caterers. She was costing him a fortune! When the guests arrived, all the gentlemen were laughing and talking about golf and right-wing politics, while the women chatted about flower arrangements, when suddenly Sarah loudly advised that she thought "Jeremy Corbyn was a bloody nice bloke". All eyes were on Sarah as she listed the virtues of the Labour Party. The men started growling and shuffling their feet, whilst the women looked bemused. One of the women tried to change the subject by saying "I know nothing about politics, but what I really like is how quickly Harrods deliver on a Friday" causing her husband to stroke her hand affectionately. Daddy was fuelled with embarrassment and bellowed "We will not have women talking about politics here, especially not supporters of the loony left!" Daddy had then stormed out to his den, pulled his shotgun from the cabinet and frog marched a screaming Sarah out of the front door. But Sarah would not go easily, banging on the windows and screaming obscenities. Daddy was forced to call his gamekeeper to escort her off the premises and arrange for her possessions to be sent on. Still this did not get rid of Sarah, who kept returning to the manor for weeks, until Daddy paid her off.

Reeling from his expensive mistake, Daddy spent most evenings in the local pub - the Tally Ho - sitting in the corner with a laptop. His gamekeeper, Johnny, had shown him the wonders of the internet, which to Daddy looked like a television screen. Johnny also introduced Daddy to the mail order bride sites. Daddy evaluated how much it would cost to hire a housekeeper as opposed to buying a bride and found buying a bride was cheaper in the long run, with the extra benefits, of course. He finally settled for a Polish beauty named Zophia. Stunningly beautiful, hardworking, a good cook and a bargain; Daddy had decided to meet with Zophia straight away. They were married within a month - he wasn't hungry anymore; he had his paper on time in the mornings and the manor was clean and tidy. Daddy was happy again.

After the disastrous conversation with Daddy, Jessica phoned Penny excitedly "Penny, I have had a letter from Rollocks solicitors. Aunt Mabel, who fled to Greece after upsetting Daddy all those years ago, has passed away and left me the sole heir of her three-star hotel in Zante!" Jessica imagined Penny swishing her long dark hair back and pouting her bee stung lips. "Darling this is wonderful!" exclaimed Penny. "Fresh Olives, Tzatziki, pitta bread, Greek salad!" Jessica read out parts of the letter "It's an all-inclusive hotel, serving breakfast, lunch and dinner, snacks. Oh, and a swimming pool, Jacuzzi and olive groves!" Penny squealed in excitement, visualising pound signs. Penny enjoyed manipulating Jessica and had, since the yoga therapy group session, had easily been able to control the woman who was now funding her lifestyle. "I assume we will have staff able to attend to us and the guests. I expect most of the holidaymakers will be expecting fresh fruit for breakfast, a light lunch of pitta and olives and dinner with the freshest seafood, all washed down with champers! When are we leaving, Jessica?" Jessica opened her laptop and searched flights from Gatwick. "I can get us flights from Gatwick tomorrow at 11:00. Don't worry about packing too much, I imagine there are numerous boutiques we can shop in". Penny hung up her phone, breathing a huge sigh of relief. This was just the escape she needed, as she had sensed that her time living off the strange and perverted Bert was coming to an end.

Jessica booked the flights and shouted to Mrs May, who was removing her coat and tying her apron around her waist. "We are off to Greece tomorrow, get packed and get that driver Carlos to pick us up at 9:30". Mrs May picked up the letter. Greece, she thought, all-inclusive Brown Ale, Bingo, Karaoke and a bit of sun. A smile crept over her face; this was just what she needed. She also needed a good laugh and the way Jessica was these days, she needed a bit of that snobbery pushed out of her. Carlos also smiled when he had the phone call from Mrs May. He had seen her from a far and always had a crush on her. There was something mysterious about Mrs May that made his legs wobble a little bit.

Jessica walked out of the large modern kitchen and entered her bedroom gazing at herself in the mirror. Not bad for forty she thought, taking in the reflection of the slim blonde-haired woman looking back at her. She then called her husband Justin, hoping he would be able to talk from his office in Tokyo. "Darling, I have news!" A sigh filled the earpiece of the phone. "How much will it cost me?" Jessica laughed "Nothing, darling. Great Aunt Mabel has passed away and left me her hotel in Greece." Justin filled the line with a belly laugh. "You? Running an all-inclusive hotel in Zante? You do know what the guests will be like?" Jessica cut in "Yes, they will be travelling for the culture of Greece, touring the olive groves, Greek food, authentic Greek dancing. It will be a journey of culture and good taste, the real Greece!" The line cleared. Justin sat back in his black leather chair, tears running down his face with laughter. Unlike Jessica, Justin had grown up on a council estate in North London before making it big as an IT executive. He knew all about all-inclusive holidays at three-star resorts and the expectations of holiday makers they attracted. Justin believed that this would teach his wife a lesson and hopefully she would return to the un snobby, kind-hearted woman he had married. Recently Jessica had become cold and cruel since - all she met that awful Penny, who leached money and happiness out of Jessica. Justin recalled his holiday with Jessica to Cuba, where they were greeted with champagne, butler service and access to a spa. Jessica was very used to the good life and had been sheltered from the world of package holidays but although naïve, she was not cruel. Justin wished he would be there to witness her reaction to the new world she was entering of fried breakfasts, chips, burgers, hot dogs and brown ale; although he knew poor long-suffering Mrs May would, at least, enjoy it. Justin decided that this was a trip he just could not miss and booked a flight to Zante straight away.

Carlos pulled the limousine up outside Jessica's Cottage. Mrs May walked along the front path, dragging an assortment of heavy suitcases with ease. Carlos marvelled as to how a woman of her age could drag so much baggage without breaking a sweat. Jessica walked out of the cottage. Carlos noted her highlighted cheekbones and bright red lips under the large sunglasses and her long blond hair pulled up into a high ponytail. Dressed in tiny tight jeans and a poncho, the boots she wore had what looked to be 3-inch spikes. She looked every part of the latest English expression he had learned 'dogs' dinner'. Carlos chuckled to himself, whilst opening the door for Jessica - who was demanding Mrs May opened a bottle of champagne. Once settled, Carlos drove off towards Penny's abode - an identical version of Jessica's cottage. Jessica lowered her sunglasses. "Has her property got smaller?" she sneered. The cottage door flew open as, in a dramatic theatrical entrance, Penny appeared. Dressed in a white shift dress exposing her lean legs, with large gold belt hanging from her tiny waist, wearing matching gold spiked heels. Her look was completed with an orange fake tan. Penny peeked over her large sunglasses, pouting and swishing her long hair like she was about to strut a catwalk and walked slowly towards the car. "Has she put on weight?" asked Jessica, crossing her jean clad legs. Carlos rolled his eyes and thought of another English word he had been taught recently 'mutton dressed as lamb'. He opened the door for Penny, but his eye wandered to Mrs May who, with exceptional speed, jumped out of the limousine and grabbed the three large suitcases, loading them with ease into the car. 'What a woman!' thought Carlos, as Mrs Mays ample thigh was revealed by her knee length dress riding up, whilst she loaded the suitcases into the boot of the car. "Darling! Have you lost weight?" Jessica exclaimed, whilst air kissing Penny. Penny smoothed down her dress "I love your eyebrows; I think the wild look is really in" Both women cast a beady eye over the other. Carlos was casting his eye over Mrs May's ample rump. 'A real woman" he thought.

As Mrs May opened the front passenger door of the limousine, she noticed Carlos, the fifty-year-old Greek driver, staring at her bosom. "Mummy issues" she thought, as she pulled her dress down, hiding her thighs and noticed Carlos watching her. He smoothed back his slick dark hair and adjusted his shirt, undoing another button to show his thick, dark chest hair. Mrs May felt a twinge of excitement. "So, Carlos, are you looking forward to driving in Greece". Carlos turned to Mrs May and held eye contact with his dark brown eyes, but it was then his twitch set in. Carlos had lived with his nervous twitch all his life - the dread of the flutter in his eye making him look to all like he was winking and the side chew of air from his mouth as if he was making to bite his shoulder. Mrs

May tried hard not to let her mouth fall open. "Yes" stammered Carlos, twitching again "I look forward to getting pissed on lager and eating kebabs". Mrs May smiled warmly "Oh yes me too, and bingo!" Carlos drove on, twitching in excitement.

CHAPTER 2

The car arrived at Gatwick airport, where Mrs May and Carlos jumped out of the car and loaded the suitcases onto a trolley. Carlos then passed the keys over for the vehicle to be stored at the airport garage. Jessica and Penny swaggered ahead by-passing the queue, much to the annoyance of the other five first class passengers waiting in line. "I have been waiting hours" growled Penny towards the queue, which erupted into shouts of disapproval. Jessica scowled at the crowd "You can tell the sort of people they are, Penny. Mrs May, can you please get my hand wipes?" Suddenly the crowd parted as an elderly male was pushed forward in his wheelchair. Jessica and Penny froze in horror as they recognised the white paper-thin skin of Frank Small, the postman "Hey up, Mrs Crewe. Doctor thought a holiday would do me good, what with my heart n' all and the war wound. An all- inclusive holiday to Greece with the missus, she won it ont bingo". With that a portly old lady appeared behind the wheelchair, sporting a tight perm. Jessica sighed in frustration, wondering how that decrepit old fraudster was able to afford a holiday at all. "By gum its 'hot in ere" Agnes bellowed, scratching her ample bottom. "Let's get you through ere so we can get that assistance buggy to take us to Weatherspoon's. I could do with a pint and a fry up." Agnes Small then pushed her husband to the front of the queue to check in. Jessica held back a silent scream. Penny stepped forward. "He is not disabled, he is the bloody postman!" Agnes Small doubled in size with anger. "He is bloody crippled from the war, you stuck up old cow!" Penny staggered back and, as the crowd gasped, a small cheer escaped from the back of the group. Frank Small was helped by the check in staff out of his wheelchair and, as the airport transport arrived, Frank took small steps, dragging his leg towards the buggy, which he was helped on to. He clutched his chest as Agnes Small clambered in. "To Weatherspoon's!" she bellowed and off they sped. The whole crowd, including Jessica and Penny, looked on in amazement. The crowd then rushed forward, leaving Jessica, Penny, Mrs May and Carlos at the back of the queue - Jessica and Penny with identical sulking pouts.

Jessica and Penny finally arrived in their first-class lounge and were sipping champagne. They had left Mrs May and Carlos in the main area for the 'other' passengers. Mrs May and Carlos immediately found Weatherspoon's and the Smalls. "Hey up loves, come sit ere" shouted Agnes, adjusting her bosom. They all sat together ordering lager and fry ups all round. "I'm right pleased you like proper breakfast and not that foreign muck, Carlos" exclaimed Frank. Carlos swallowed his fried bread and answered. "Hey, I like Greek muck too!" Carlos giggled to himself. 'Bloody English, he was Greek' he thought. Having the name Carlos, people always assumed he was Spanish; his mother was Spanish and his father had been Greek. He had lived most of his life in England, after moving from Greece when he was eighteen with his Mother and two sisters, not long after the breakdown of his mother's marriage. Mrs May brushed his leg under the table, causing the first tingling of a twitch. Agnes licked her lips - thinking Carlos was winking at her - turning her head away in a coy gesture, just as the twitch took over Carlos's mouth. Agnes glowed inside. 'Young lad fancies me, I still got it' she thought, running her fingers through her tight perm and looking back, offering Carlos a sneaky wink. Carlos looked back at her in abject horror, he felt his eye twitching and left the table with a final twitch, excusing himself for the bathroom. Agnes gave him an exaggerated wink as he ran towards the toilets. Frank raised his fork, waving bacon in the air. "It's the English food, I 'spect, not used to it". Mrs May put her fork down. "But he has lived in England for years!" Frank waved the bacon even higher. "Mind you, they do a right good food in Benidorm, don't they, Agnes?" Agnes lifted her pint with misty eyes. "Eye love, we 'ad that right good scran whilst watching sticky Vicky in that club, pulling the flags of all nations and a rabbit out of her fanny. Lucky, we ate first, it whiffed a bit in that club after." Mrs May didn't really want to hear what else sticky Vicky pulled out of nether regions that night and nor did the table next to them, who gave disapproving looks, which Agnes and Frank were completely oblivious to.

Ray Norman sat in the corner of Wetherspoons. It was a miracle he had got there at all, as Ray refused to admit he had trouble with his hearing and needed another eye test. He was quite happy with the pebble thick glasses he had worn for the last twenty years. Ray was a confirmed bachelor and enjoyed life frequenting pubs, where he insisted on drinking a pint of Harveys Beer in a jug, not a pint glass. He also liked going horse and dog racing. In his youth he had been a great footballer and had worked as an accountant, where he had met his friend Mick and his family. Sadly, Mick had passed away and Ray and Mick's widow, Jen, became great friends and frequently met for lunches and holidays. Ray and Jen had been looking forward to their holiday in Zante - neither had been before and were both looking forward to a new adventure. They had arranged to meet at the coffee shop at the airport. Ray had stumbled onto the wrong train after not seeing or hearing the announcements at the station. He was adamant that there had not been an announcement that the train did not stop at Gatwick, even though the guard advised him that there had been three announcements at the station and a board with a written warning. He had ended up at London Victoria and, after arguing with the guard, was put on a train that would take him to Gatwick. Finally he arrived at Gatwick, where Jen was frantically waving at him to get his attention. Ray didn't see her at first but after five minutes of waving and shouts of his name, they finally checked their luggage in and made for Wetherspoons for breakfast. The waitress arrived at their table to take their order. "How would you like your eggs - fried poached or scrambled?" Ray looked at her "Yes, I would like eggs." The waitress repeated "How would you like them?" Jen looked at Ray, "She is asking how you want your eggs". Ray looked at them both and laughed. "Yes, I like eggs". Jen addressed the confused waitress, "Give him fried, please, and I will have the poached." The waitress went off and returned a few minutes later with their breakfasts. "You have poached eggs, how did you get them, Jen, I have fried." Jen lifted her knife and fork "They gave us an option, Ray." Ray looked puzzled "I didn't hear her give us an option. I would have had the scrambled." Jen and Ray ate their breakfast; Jen carefully listening out for the announcements to board the plane as she knew Ray would end up in Australia and not Zante, if she didn't guide him in the right direction.

Meanwhile Jessica and Penny were busy discussing their business plan for the hotel. "So is there a spa?" asked Penny, looking at her freshly manicured nails. "I don't think so, we need to get one built. I can't go without my lashes or manicure or massage" replied Jessica, sipping her champagne. "Sun rise yoga is essential, I can't imagine any guests wanting to miss out on early morning stretches." Penny said "I need some nibbles, maybe some low fat, gluten free tapenade and celery." Jessica called the waitress over and ordered the food. "I didn't realise you wanted a heavy breakfast, Penny" Jessica simpered over her growling stomach. "I had a spinach smoothie for breakfast, I'm full." Her stomach growled once again. The waitress brought the minuscule plate of celery and tapenade over and placed it on the table in front of them. The waitress then returned to the corner of the champagne bar, where she could not be seen, and observed the two middle aged ladies picking at celery. She bit into her buttery bacon sandwich, stretching out her thin legs. Just as she was taking another bite, she heard "Waitress". Oh god the gruesome twosome were calling again! She skipped over, to find the dark-haired gargoyle waving her arm "At last! I need more celery. "The waitress raised her eyebrows and walked away to prepare the celery. Whilst in earshot Jessica loudly whispered "She is huge, she must be a size ten! And look at her hair, mousey and lank." Penny answered in a loud whisper "Cheap shoes, she will never make anything of herself. Just shows youth is not always beauty."

The waitress entered the kitchen, chopped the celery

and, in a fit of anger she then spat on it, wiping the saliva up and down each piece. "Have that, bitch queens from hell" she said under her breath, as she fixed a smile on her face and placed the celery down in front of them. The waitress then walked back to her hidden corner and watched the sisters savouring every bit of the celery, filling the her with a warm glow. I will take that modelling contract I have been offered, she decided and picked up the phone to Star modelling agency. Jessica chomped down onto a piece of celery and savoured the salty, delicate flavour "Is that bacon I can taste?" she asked Penny. "It does have a nice tang to it, maybe it's a new Himalayan salt added to flavour it." They both chomped on the celery and sipped the champagne, whilst the waitress looked on with a warm fuzzy feeling in her stomach.

Frank scraped his plate and licked his knife, letting out a burp that drowned out the surrounding diner's conversations. "Pardon" he shouted. "Better out than in, love" said Agnes, lifting her ample bottom off the seat. "It's polite in some countries to burp, innit?" Mrs May looked at Frank with dismay. "Where did you hear that, Frank?" Frank scratched his head "I don't right know, but I know them foreigners have funny ideas - some don't even like bacon! I travelled me, in my war days." Agnes looked aghast. "Don't like bacon? Trendy vegetarians I bet, I have eaten meat all my life and there is nowt wrong with me." Frank turned to Agnes "Oh by gum, you like a good sausage. Remember when you won the woman's champion sausage scoffing competition 'int village? I have never known a woman to scoff so much sausage in my life. Still don't know how you fit it all in. I knew when I saw that, that you were the woman for me, eye." Carlos looked on in disgust. "Sausage eating?" questioned Carlos. "YES" shouted Frank, motioning eating a sausage. "You know, sausage in mouth, yum!" Carlos looked puzzled. "See these foreigners, it's not their fault, you just have to shout a bit for them to understand you." Carlos thought 'bloody English, sex mad'. The thought of Agnes with a sausage sent a cold sweat down his back. Mrs May stifled a laugh as the nearby tables were fixated on Franks unintended filatio motion and talk of sausage. Mrs May looked up at the board. "Our flight is ready for boarding" she said, in a soft voice, aware that the surrounding diners were watching them. Frank limped along to the airport buggy, followed by Agnes. "See you ont plane!" Frank called across to Mrs May and Carlos, who waved back to them. Agnes gave an exaggerated wink to Carlos as the buggy moved off, much to the dismay of Carlos who desperately looked at the floor, trying to control the twitching in his eye.

"That's the announcement" said Jen. "Was it, Jen, I didn't hear it" said Ray, polishing off the last of his toast. "Was it ncement, Jen, really?" Jen looked at Ray "Yes, gate 3."

ı. "What gate is it, Jen?" Jen got up from the table, leading the way, whilst Ray looked at the board but could not see gate 3. Jen followed the crowds with Ray. "How do you know where gate 3 is, Jen?" Jen continued walking. "I'm following the signs, Ray." Ray stood next to the big arrow sign for gate 3. "I can't see any signs" he said. Jen laughed to herself. She had learned over the years to be Ray's eyes and ears, guiding him across roads and warning him of steps. Ray would insist that there was nothing wrong with his hearing or his eyesight and maintained that he didn't need help.

CHAPTER 3

Carlos and Mrs May followed the crowds to gate 3; the herd-like mentality took over as the gate opened to board the plane and the crowd pushed forward. Whilst waiting patiently in the queue, Mrs May recognised the loud snobby voice of Jessica. "First class here, let us through." The Cabin crew stood forward to greet Jessica and Penny and to escort them onto the plane. Suddenly there was a screech of airport buggy brakes and a booming voice. "Hey up! Disabled first class ere!" Agnes was waving her ample arm to the cabin crew, who immediately ran forward with a wheelchair to assist Frank. He stumbled off the buggy into a waiting wheelchair. Jessica let out a screech that silenced the crowds. "We were here first! He is a bloody postman, he is not first class and he is not disabled." Agnes approached Jessica and Penny, who seemed to shrink in size compared to her ample frame. "Shut up, you heartless old cow, look at you two! Won't let a harmless crippled bloody war hero get on the plane first, you should be ashamed of yourself." Jessica stood open mouthed as a voice came from the crowd. "Poor old man, what a horrible cow!" The crowd started muttering and hurling abuse at Jessica and Penny. "Old trout!" "Stuck up cow!" "Ugly old munter!" Jessica turned to Penny. "Old! They called me old! What's a munter?" Penny patted Jessica's small arm "I expect it's a working-class word, you know poor people's slang or cockney." Jessica and Penny were pushed aside as Frank was wheeled forward to get on the plane, followed by Agnes who was still muttering "Stuck up old bitch". Jessica watched as yet again, Frank bypassed the queue. "Penny, I need champagne, get me on that plane." Penny waved to the cabin crew, who avoided eye contact, and ignored every attempt made to gain their attention.

Simone could see the two woman waving frantically at the corner of her eye. 'You can wait' she thought. 'Teach you to be horrible to that poor old man.' Simone had worked as cabin crew for ten years, dealing with numerous difficult spoilt bitches and, from the description her daughter Daisy, who worked in the first class lounge had given her of the two gargoyles who had called her fat, Simone was sure they were one and the same. Simone let them wave and shout for another few minutes, until she strolled over to them. "At last! We are first class and I have one of my stress headaches coming on, I need to get on that plane and rest" said Jessica, in a high-pitched voice. Simone looked them up and down. 'I will serve you, alright' she thought, as she invited them to follow her. Simone hated Daisy being upset and took on the role of a Tiger protecting her cubs when anyone upset her. Besides, Daisy had been offered a modelling contract and would soon be gracing the front pages of the magazines that sat on the coffee tables of rich bitches like these two. She would dearly love to see the faces of those two ageing stick insects when Daisy made it in the modelling world.

Carlos and Mrs May settled themselves in their seats. Mrs May reflected on her time before the accident, when she travelled the world with the other World's Strongest woman contestants. She lulled herself to sleep, dreaming of the day she had the title "Hurricane May". Clad in a leopard print bikini, she had travelled the world, parading up and down the stages and receiving standing ovations for her numerous weightlifting achievements. Well, some standing achievements, there seemed to always be a row of males at the front, with newspapers on their laps, fixed grins on their faces and a lot of shuffling. Carlos tried to remove Mrs May's head from his shoulder - not only was her drool seeping through his shirt but the ear defying snorts emitting from her mouth and nose were akin to a rutting warthog. Carlos attempted to give Mrs May a good nudge. This only resulted in Mrs May's head dropping straight into the lap of a twitching Carlos. This caused Carlos great anxiety as part of him quite liked Mrs May's head bobbing up and down on his lap, but he could also see other passengers looking at them; some appeared to be giggling and some were looking disgusted. Then, just as he had feared the air hostess started walking along the plane towards him, checking the seat belts.

Simone began walking up and down the plane to check that all the safety belts were assembled ready for take-off. She was called over by a passenger. "'Ere love, there's some funny business going on over there." Simone looked over the seat and recoiled in horror at the twitching face of Carlos and the bobbing head of Mrs May's head in his lap. Simone grabbed a rolled up newspaper and trotted towards them shouting "You can pack that up!" Carlos looked mortified as he frantically tried to explain. "It's not what you think, she's sleeping! Snoring like a snuffling pig!" Mrs May let out a snore of mighty proportions. Simone jumped back in fright "I'm watching you both, no funny business" she said, shaking her newspaper at them to the amusement of the passengers around her. Simone knew what some of the passengers could be like. It was only last week that she had caught a couple desperate to join the mile-high club, behind a makeshift tent out of blankets. Simone had caught several randy couples in her time and decided that no one would be putting their tents up on her flights again.

Ray and Jen got comfortable in their seats. "I didn't hear the announcement" said Ray. Jen recalled the time she went on holiday with Ray to Blackpool. Ray had been determined all holiday to buy a stick of rock to take home for his niece. Ray had told Jen that he had been out and about and not seen any rock anywhere. Jen was surprised by this as she saw rock and 'kiss me quick' hats everywhere. Jen walked Ray to a shop that was called 'The Rock Shop' and was famous in Blackpool for its huge selection of rock. Jen entered the shop and was amazed by all the colours and different types of rock that were stacked floor to ceiling on display shelves. She saw Ray at the counter buying a postcard. As she followed him out of the shop, she asked him why he hadn't bought any rock. Ray told her that he was surprised that the shop didn't sell rock. Jen had laughed and pointed out it was floor to ceiling rock. Ray could not understand why he had only got a postcard. Jen couldn't really understand either, but accepted Ray would be the only person in the history of the world to enter a shop full of what he wanted and not see any of it! Jen saw the drinks trolley coming along the aisle and waved frantically at the stewardess. "Large red wine "she gasped. She took a deep gulp of wine, as Ray ordered a beer. Jen had known Ray for a very long time. She had spent many years being entertained by Rays un- knowingly hilarious antics. Jen had brought the pocket version of 'Who Wants to be a Millionaire' and they both decided to play. Jen asked Ray the question – 'If you have a problem in your neighbourhood, who are you going to call?'

A-The police

B-The Council

C-Ghostbusters

D-The vet

Ray answered B! Jen started laughing "No, Ray, it's Ghostbusters, like the film." Ray thought this was nonsense and was adamant that if you have a problem in your neighbourhood, you would always call the Council. The more Ray said this, the more Jen laughed. The more Jen laughed, the more adamant Ray became. Ray then huffed that it was 'a silly game' and started reading his paper. Jen snuggled down in her seat and started reading her book 'The World's Worst Serial Killers.' She looked around the passengers, inspecting their hairstyles and shoes and any other tell signs that they might be murderers. She had noticed that serial killers did tend to have a certain hairstyle, usually with a sharp side parting and brothel creeper shoes. Looking around, she saw plenty of candidates and as she snuck a final look, flipped to the next book chapter, which was all about Ted Bundy.

Jessica and Penny sat in their seats in stony silence, watching Frank and Agnes get handed champagne. "Ooh the bubbles go right up my nose, mind you these small glasses are like drinking out of a thimble" Agnes hiccupped, staring around at the other first class passengers. "Here Frank, seems like they need a bit of livening up in ere, like a bloody morgue!" Frank looked around the plane and noticed the businessmen reading their papers and the stony faces of Jessica Crewe and her stuck-up friend, Penny Beech. Miserable old cows, he thought. Being the local postman, Frank knew all the local gossip and habits of the villagers of Lealands this was mostly due to collecting the mail from the post office in the morning and then swiftly returning home to Agnes, who had the kettle steaming, ready to open and read all the letters,. Often, Frank would read out extracts from the letters to Agnes, who claimed to be psychic in the village and could tell you your fortune for a price. Agnes had earned herself a fifty quid from Jessica a few years ago when Jessica wanted to find out if she would be having a brother or sister. Agnes had got confused opening the letters addressed to Jessica's mother and the heavily pregnant Mrs Wyatt. It turned out that Mrs Wyatt was pregnant with a girl and Jessica's Mother with a boy. She had told Jessica she would have a sister. Agnes had never been asked back to the cottage since. Jessica Crewe and Penny Beech were not as posh as they made out to be, especially after reading the filthy letters to the plumber Penny had sent. It was also rumoured around the village that Burt, Penny's fancy man, was a bit of a strange character and was hardly seen around the village. Frank knew that Penny was not married to Burt and it was rumoured that Burt had been in prison for some sort of obscene flashing episode and was on some sort of register.

Simone plied Frank and Agnes with champagne, as she felt sorry for the old veteran who was injured fighting all over the world and wanted to make his competition winning holiday one to remember. The champagne seemed to be doing the trick, as Frank started singing "WERE ALL GOING 'ONT SUMMER 'OLIDAY", causing the businessman in the row behind to look over his copy of the Telegraph in disgust. Agnes joined in enthusiastically, causing more and more startled responses of passengers shaking their newspapers and coughing loudly. Agnes looked over the crowded plane and spotted Jessica and Penny cringing in their seats. "Hey Mrs Crewe, did your Doctor's Appointment go other week?" Jessica felt her cheeks redden. Jessica had made an appointment with Dr Prevo or, as he was known in the village, Dr *Pervoooooh* due to him expelling a large "ooooh" when he performed an examination. Jessica had seen him about a lump on her bottom.

Dr Prevo much preferred examining young men and insisted on full body check- ups whenever they went into the surgery. He had looked Jessica up and down with disgust and told her to go for a jolly good walk to sort out her hysteria. Prevo particularly enjoyed examining a young builder who was shocked when asked to remove his clothes when he only had a sore finger. "Come on, all boys together, no fillies" said Prevo, his hands wandering over naked flesh. Prevo had been disgusted by having to examine both Jessica and Penny regarding their woman's complaints and rushed them both out as fast as he could, when he noticed a young buck named Andy waiting to be seen. Andy had not heard about the incident with the builder and felt he was getting good service when first rushed into the Doctor's room. Andy explained that he had a sore throat and achy muscles. Prevo gave a long "ooooh" as he asked Andy to remove all his clothes, leaving him in only his socks. Andy sat in the chair feeling cold and a bit embarrassed "Don't worry, all boys together, no damn fillies" said Prevo breathing hard into Andy's ear. It was at this point Andy realised he really should not be naked in a small room with Dr Prevo "Don't be embarrassed, we all have them, us men, you know…penises "Andy quickly pulled his clothes on and made for the door, fumbling with the handle to get out. He raced out of the room and into the waiting area, still dressing, being chased by Prevo. It was then that Prevo spotted Bert who turned up at the clinic every day, sitting gazing at Prevo, who stopped in his tracks with a look of fear on his face. Bert got up and skipped into the office "Shall I get my kit off, Doctor?" and promptly unzipped his trousers. "Same as yesterday, Bert, just add the wart cream and it will go." Bert sloped out of the clinic with a sad expression, calling back "see you tomorrow." Dr Prevo didn't know what he hated more - damn women or Bert and his warty penis.

Penny's appointment was to discuss her urine infection - that had been ongoing since she had her regrettable affair with Georgio the plumber some months ago. Georgio, with his olive skin and seductive Italian accent, had swept Penny off her feet. Penny had never felt any affection for a man, but there was something about him that she was attracted to, even though he was poor. She had found out that Georgio had a few wealthy women he was seeing at the same time. It was when Georgio had told Penny he needed money to help his mother in Italy and then they could elope together, that things starting to become regrettable. Penny transferred thousands of pounds into his mother's bank account only to never hear from him again. She had written countless letters to him, unwilling to believe he would not return to her. Penny had immediately vowed to hunt Georgio down and feed him to the pigs, but every lead she followed to find him came to a dead end.

Jessica looked away and said "Fine" in a small voice, hoping she would not reveal she had a lump on her bottom to all the first- class passengers. Agnes continued, "This is the thing with them plumbers, forever sticking it where it shouldn't be, could do with it being cut off. I hear even old Sheila Cobb's 'ad a go. Poor old cow. Hear she'd never had an organism before, I don't know what an organism is, but she said she couldn't walk for a week after. She says she hasn't been able to get a plumber as good since." Jessica did not know what Agnes was talking about, but cringed further at the thought of old Miss Cobbs with her musty old cat hair covered cardigan, tartan skirt with white socks and brown sandals; the veins in her legs popping out along with the hairs. She had the distinct smell of corned beef and insisted she did not need to use her hearing aid as "she could hear a pin drop" without it on. Numerous complaints had been made about the blaring noise from her television and radio. One terrible night she fell asleep whilst leaving Basic Instinct on. The whole street could hear Sharon Stone romping away for two hours, Jessica shuddered at the thought of that being Mrs Cobbs with the plumber. Penny looked a little green and thought back to the day Georgio left a grey curly short hair in the bathroom soap. Georgio insisted it was a cat hair at the time. Surely it would not be possible to have sex with Mrs Cobb at her age, as her bits must have healed up or have been full of cobwebs. Penny vowed never to fall for a man again.

The surrounding passengers looked on with their mouths gaping open, as Agnes then stood up and attempted to open the window "It's right hot in ere" she said wiping her brow "Can't get bloody window open." Simone calmly walked over and showed Agnes how to use the air conditioning. Frank turned to the crowd and let out a rip-roaring belch "PARDON, that's champagne that is!" The passengers continued to watch in stunned silence, until a middle aged lady turned to Jessica "I am terribly sorry, but can you ask your parents to quieten down a bit - they are rather loud and vulgar" Jessica sat upright "They aren't my parents, he is a bloody postman and she is the village psychic! I don't know them" Then the voice of Agnes loudly exclaimed "VULGAR, BLOODY VULGAR? HEAR THAT FRANK? YOU NOSEY OLD BITCH, HE IS A WAR HERO, YOU SHOULD BE BLOODY THANKING 'IM! Got more class than you in my butthole, lady" The lady looked down her nose with contempt. "You come on a first class flight that, quite frankly, looking at you, you can't afford and talk about sex and burp like a gurgling hog and you talk about class? Honestly you northerners need a lesson in manners and courtesy." Agnes walked along the plane towards the lady, rolling up her sleeves and folding her arms. "I know your type, all fur coat and no knickers, look at state of you, sitting there with a face like a bulldog chewing a wasp, smelling like your gudgeon's gone off. I tell you, lady, you need to pull your head out of your arse and shut up or we can make summit of it in Greece when we land." The lady shrunk back into her seat.

Frank looked on at his wife, his heart bursting with love, 'that's my girl' he thought 'won't take any nonsense her, she is a fighter is Agnes'. Frank chuckled over a memory of Agnes last year, being told by the milkman she had not paid her bill. She had marched straight up to his van, pulled off a crate of milk and thrown it at the milkman shouting "now sod off". The posh passenger sloped away, telling the passengers that standards had dropped in first class, as they let anyone on now. She sat down on her seat next to her cringing husband, asking, "Isn't a gudgeon a fish?" Her husband muttered a quiet "think so" and pleaded for her to not engage again. His wife crossed her arms and sulked throughout the rest of the journey. Agnes walked back to her seat "bloody cheek." Frank stroked her hand "Don't you worry my pet, nearly in Greece, away from these snobby buggers." With that the plane prepared for landing.

Justin Crewe arrived at the Olive Grove Hotel. The receptionist checked him in, and he casually carried his bag up to his basic, but modern room. He changed into his shorts and decided to go for a swim in the lovely outdoor pool that was situated next to the bar. Justin sauntered down to the pool and jumped into the gloriously cold water, surrounded by families on lidos having fun and guests of all ages sitting around the pool enjoying ice creams and the sun. What looked to be a stag party were playing a drinking game by the pool, downing numerous shots shouting, "One for his nob" and roaring with laughter. Justin dried off, ordered a white wine at the bar and waited for the grand entrance of his wife Jessica. Justin tasted the wine, which was very rough, so he downed it quickly to be polite and then ordered a tequila sunrise from the friendly barmaid. Jessica had changed in the last few months; she had lost weight and become obsessed with her appearance. He had tried to advise Jessica that Penny was leeching her money and changing Jessica into a cruel and heartless person. Jessica constantly defended Penny, making allowances for her rudeness and her shallow love for herself and money. Justin also felt very uncomfortable around Penny, who he was sure was trying to seduce him, giving him flirty little winks and dropping items in front of him. She did a lot of bending forward in a short skirt to pick things up and Justin was pretty sure she had picked a lot of things up in her time, probably being prescribed very strong antibiotics to get rid of said things. He knew Penny's kind - money grabbing strumpets set on taking every penny. Justin hoped that one day he would pluck up the courage to demand that Jessica end their friendship. He didn't want it to come to demanding who she was friends with, as he wasn't a controlling man, but he really wanted to heave Penny out of their lives once and for all. He had a horrible feeling that Penny would be arriving at the hotel with Jessica, travel all paid for with their money. Justin sipped his cocktail, admiring the attractive women around him of all shapes and sizes, laughing and drinking pints. Jessica would never drink a pint and rarely laughed unless it was at the misfortune of another female these days. He yearned for the Jessica he met to return to him.

Justin had arranged to meet the vicar, Meek, who had offered to conduct the funeral for Mabel, to discuss the arrangements in the pool bar in twenty minutes. He carried on drinking his cocktail and then heard rautious laughter and a scream from the other side of the bar. Justin stood up to get a better view, to see a portly vicar sitting on a barstool. The screaming female walked quickly past Justin, muttering to her friend," that vicar pinched my bum." Justin, along with both girls, looked across to the vicar, who raised his butt cheek and let out a rip-roaring fart, winking at the girls, who ran off. Justin chuckled - he couldn't believe what he had just seen. He then heard the strong Irish accent of Meek order another whiskey and noticed him swaying on the barstool. He seemed to be telling the patient barmaid about the craic he had last week in that very chair. Crack, thought Justin, surely he doesn't mean drugs? Justin approached Meek and introduced himself. He was swiftly invited to sit down, while Meek ordered two whiskeys. Justin found it difficult to decipher what he was saying, due to Meek's level of intoxication and strong accent; however between whiskeys he managed to pick up certain words "Mabel, loved the craic, fine woman" and "The lads in the Irish football are doing well." Justin arranged to meet Meek at his church the next day, hoping that he would be able to make funeral arrangements with a sober Meek. Justin left Meek propped up at the bar, singing along with the stag party.

Justin walked into the reception area, just as he heard the clipping heels and the barked orders from Jessica to Mrs May. Jessica had clearly not enjoyed her journey from the airport to the hotel "There is rubbish all along that road, buildings unfinished and the hire car was an old Yaris and it stunk of fish" She started frantically smelling her clothes and shouting "Fish! Penny and I have never travelled like that in our lives." Penny gave a scathing look and sniffed. "I thought this was going to be a grand affair, Jessica. It seems we have arrived in a poor people's hostel. I didn't realise people lived like this"

Jessica started frantically apologising to Penny, promising things would get better.

Anna the receptionist looked over her desk and saw the skeletal forms of Jessica and Penny, who clipped across the tiles. She noted the lady with the strong calf muscles dragging the suitcases, whilst a large Greek male hid in the shadows of the reception area. Jessica lowered her sunglasses, along with Penny, a look of horror taking over their faces. "Welcome" said Anna "Champagne, I need Champagne, cold. Mrs May, can you wipe that seat so Penny and I can sit down?" demanded Jessica. Anna looked at Jessica with a large smile. "No Champagne on the island. Same for all the island. Go to the bar and get a cocktail - screaming orgasm is good." Jessica staggered back. "No Champagne, screaming orgasm?" Anna nodded enthusiastically. "Yes Illios, he makes best screaming orgasm." A portly female waddled past in a skimpy bikini, shouting at her toddler. "Dylan, you little sod, I told you no more bloody slush puppies - they make you piss in the pool!" Jessica and Penny looked like they might faint. Jessica then noticed Justin watching them. She tottered up to him in her heels "Darling, help me! I have been in hell since I left England" Jessica didn't notice the look of contempt on his handsome face, his blue eyes filled with hatred directed at Penny, who was oblivious and turning her nose up at the lounge decor. Justin held Jessica's hands. "You must feel dreadful" Jessica stared at him "I know! They don't have champagne, and I am surrounded by fat people. That horrible receptionist said a barman will give me an orgasm and I don't want one." Justin sighed. "No, Jessica, about Aunt Mabel." Jessica screwed up her face "I bet she just wanted to spite me, has she left me anything, apart from this ramshackle hovel?".

CHAPTER 4

Aunt Mabel had reached the grand age of 88 before her passing, she was well known on the island as "the Godmother" on account of her shady deals and links to the Mafia. Since humiliating her brother in the gentleman's club, she had started a new life in Zante and became a poker shark, frequenting casinos and winning against the house. Mabel was known for her cigar smoking poker face and had numerous admirers. Her head was only turned once and that was by Charlie Crook, who resembled his surname in every way. Charlie had seen potential in Mabel straight away and informed the big Mafioso boss that the poker playing Mabel would be cleaning up in Casinos and poker games all over the world, and, as such would be a great business investment for the mob. As the romance between Charlie and Mabel blossomed, they travelled the world together, cleaning out casinos and bringing home large profits for herself and the Mafia. Mabel, although still a strong feminist, settled into the life of being a gangster's mole. She thought very little these days of her family back in England, only sending the occasional letter to her niece Jessica, who Mabel believed was as daft as a brush - but the best of a bad bunch. Mabel had retired from poker at the grand age of seventy and then lived a life of luxury. Her poker days had secured her a large house on the island of Zantea three star hotel called 'The Olive Groves' and lifelong protection from the Mafia.

Mabel fell in love with the hotel instantly and spent many happy hours around the pool, enjoying the company of the regular customers. She tried to bring new life into the hotel, but soon found the customers liked the hotel just the way it was, with its entertainment and mixture of Greek and British food. Although Mabel had a fearsome reputation on the island with enemies of the Mafia, she had a very kind side. Charlie and Mabel lived happily together, until Charlie made the terrible mistake of having an affair with Doris, who worked on the meat counter in the local supermarket. Both knew they were playing a dangerous game meeting up in the back of the meat van for a quick romp. Knowing the danger of their situation, they would take their cars to remote locations for a furtive fumble. This seemed to work well for a while, until the fateful day Charlie was thrusting into Doris in the back of his car, when he was distracted by the sound or a large engine. Both he and Doris were dismayed to see a coach full of tourists pull up next to them, the faces of shocked tourists staring down at them. Charlie felt shooting pains running up his arm and into his chest, causing him to collapse on top of Doris, trapping her under him. Doris screamed for help as the coach roared away. She lay there for hours with the corpse of Charlie on top of her, his face fixed in a mad grin. Eventually after passing out, she woke to hear a vehicle pull up.

Officer Carras had spent the afternoon in his favourite Taverna, feeling rather merry after his pint of Methos, the local beer. He had ignored his police radio for the last hour, as he usually did in the afternoons but now he finally stretched out his long arms and answered the frantic calls from the control room to his radio. Carras was not surprised to hear that a sexual act was being performed in a car at the remote beauty spot on the Island. 'It will be the English', he thought. Although Carras welcomed tourists to the Island, as long as they behaved, he had a dislike for the English that were buying up the properties on the Island and working, taking the jobs away from the locals and forcing fish and chips on everyone. 'Give it ten years' he thought, and they would be overrun with English. He was sure there was a conspiracy with the Greek government that allowed the English to buy up the properties and businesses before the locals did and they were plotting the invasion of Greece.

Officer Carras slowly walked to his patrol car and set off. He arrived half an hour later, to his disappointment the vehicle was still there but, as he approached slowly, he heard a faint scream. As he opened the door of the suspect vehicle, exclaiming "filthy pigs", his eyes fell on the scene of horror in front of him. Sixty-year-old Doris - from the meat counter - was stuck beneath what looked to be the corpse of Mr Charlie, husband of the Godmother. The scene would traumatise Carras for years. The sight of Doris's hairy, veiny legs gripped around the dead thighs of Mr Charlie, who had a manic grin on his face. Rigor mortis appeared to have set in, and the afternoon heat had caused the body to start to decompose, causing the air to be filled with an unpleasant aroma of rotting eggs, stale cabbage and fish. Carras took this as proof that the English really did all smell of fish and chips.

He radioed the control room at the police station, who immediately sent response cars and an ambulance to the scene. The media reported it was the fastest response on the Greek island that had ever been known. Back up arrived in the form of three police cars, two ambulances and a fire engine, followed by the local news stations reporting live from the scene. A local entrepreneur had hired two coaches and charged tourists ten euros each to be taken to the scene for a bird's eye view of the action. Numerous food trucks showed up selling gyros and ice cream to the fascinated tourists, who watched whilst stuffing their faces as the fire brigade sawed through the roof of the car with chainsaws. Eventually a crane lifted the roof of the car off, as paramedics attempted to lift the rotting corpse of Charlie off of the distressed Doris, who was in and out of consciousness. One final heave from the paramedics pulled Charlie off Doris, the sound of clapping thunder filled the scene, as the air from Charlies body erupted, loosening his bowels, which sprayed back over the screaming Doris.

Carras was tasked with visiting Mabel and passing on the death message. Carras was always being reminded by his wife Helen to be more sympathetic, especially towards the tourists, as they kept him in a job. He didn't mind Mabel being English on the Island, as she targeted the English business with the Mafia protection rackets. She also gave rather large bribes and pay outs to the police officers to turn a blind eye to various misdemeanours and crimes that occurred on the Island. He arrived at her villa, to be greeted by two large henchmen, who led him through the large villa to Mabel, who was lying by the ample swimming pool. Mabel removed her sunglasses. "Officer Carras welcome, I believe you have news of my husband, please sit down." Carras sat down next to Mabel, removing his hat "You already know?" She nodded. "Yes, it has been broadcast on every news network on the TV and radio on the Island." Carras shuffled his feet "This is the consequence of woofing, I'm afraid." Mabel asked "Do you mean dogging?" Carras nodded "No good will come of woofing". Carras could never quite understand why the English insisted on woofing - he cleared many a tourist away from remote areas, hoping they would not return.

Mabel watched Officer Carras drive off in his patrol car. She couldn't quite decide if she was broken hearted or angry. Charlie wasn't a saint by any stretch of the imagination but he had never been unfaithful before. Mabel then began plotting her revenge on Doris, the old trollop would not get away with her affair with Charlie. Charlie had got what was coming to him, Doris was next. Mabel devised a plan to befriend Doris and then ensure she had a painful death when she least expected it. She picked up her telephone and called the hospital to enquire as to how Doris was. The nurse reported she was doing well and would be discharged the next day; Mabel hung up the phone grinning.

Doris lay in the hospital reflecting upon the previous day, when a nurse plonked a newspaper on her hospital bed. The front-page headline "Man dies in car, on top of saucy mistress" taunted her. Numerous journalists were competing to obtain an interview with Doris, who had to be moved to a hospital ward on the third floor of the hospital, to escape those taking photos through the window and trying to get in. One desperate journalist had sneaked into the hospital and stolen a nurse's uniform and crept into Doris's room, waking Doris from her slumber. Doris screamed as her sleepy eyes fell upon a six-foot portly male, with meaty hairy arms and a poorly fitted wig hushing her. The journalist said "Tell me about the woofing and

Mr Charlie." Doris jumped out of bed, striking the pose of a crouching tiger, causing the journalist to cower in the corner of the room whimpering. "You can sod off" screamed Doris, springing forward, her night gown rising revealing her flowered bloomers. The journalist had not accounted for Doris being so lively on her feet, or so ferocious. Doris started walking towards him, slowly pulling the sleeves of her dressing gown up. The journalist ran from the ward, screeching in terror leaving the ungainly black wig behind. Doris quickly picked up the wig and stuck it in her bloomers 'might come in useful later', she thought 'waste not want not'. She had a feeling that Mabel would arrive looking for revenge. Doris was ready, as what a lot of people didn't realise about Doris, was she was a black belt in Karate and prided herself on her ability to fight to the death if need be. Growing up in the east end of London, and having five brothers, Doris was no stranger to having a scrap and quite enjoyed it. She had moved to Greece many moons ago for a new life, after selling the family pie stall business and craving some sunshine.

A robust nurse entered Doris's room "All ok, Miss Doris?" Doris looked across at her "Yes dear, just very tired" The nurses eyes adjusted to the light. Doris was lying with her nightgown lifted, showing her bloomers. Her eye caught a large bulge at the front of the flowery bloomers. She was also sure that she could see long hair hanging out the sides of them. The nurse wrinkled her nose, wishing that Doris had the decency to shave. It looked like a haystack down there, Charlie must have needed a hedge cutter to get through that shredded wheat. There is more to this story with Mr Charlie, she thought.

The next morning, Mabel put her plan in to action. Purchasing a large bunch of flowers, she made her way to the hospital - poisoned dart hidden within the flowers and blowpipe in the inside pocket of her long camel coat. She took the lift to the ward on the third floor and, when she reached the room with Doris inside, asked her henchmen to ensure that no one entered. Mabel then crept into the room. Doris had been expecting Mabel and was pretending to be asleep. As Mabel approached the bed Doris jumped up, standing on the bed, Doris looked Mabel up and down. "You took your time." Mabel smiled "I knew you would be expecting me" Mabel quickly drew the blowpipe fixed the dart in an expertly fashion, wrapping her lips around the pipe. As quick as a flash Doris jumped up, drawing a flick knife from the waistband of her bloomers. The shock caused Mabel to breathe in swallowing the poisoned dart. Mabel coughed away, while Doris quickly dressed and put on the saved wig. She expertly made a long rope from the bedding and escaped out of the window, disguised in a wig and wearing Mabel's long Camel coat, never to be seen again - much to the disappointment of the journalists who had gone home for the evening. The police had described the incident as foul play and could not understand how Mabel had swallowed the dart and how Doris had escaped. This added to the media frenzy already surrounding the circumstances.

CHAPTER 5

Anna, the receptionist at the hotel, offered to show Jessica and Penny their room. "Penthouse I assume, I do hope we are not sharing" said Penny, sticking her nose up. Anna looked confused "Yes you share, the penthouse suite is taken by big competition winner and war hero." Jessica burst into tears, Anna attempted to comfort her. "Of course, you are upset about Mrs Mabel, we make nice funeral reception here." Anna patted Jessica's shoulder "I am upset because I am stuck in this dump, all I can smell is chip fat and I am going to have to stay here amongst people whose idea of sophistication is stuffing disgusting burgers in their mouths and drinking foul cocktails. Rabble, the lot of them." Justin rolled his eyes while Jessica inspected the sheets and screamed "I hope there are not cheap sheets, my skin won't cope." Penny, never one to miss an opportunity to snipe at Jessica, advised that Jessica's skin was quite leathery, so she probably wouldn't notice. Jessica looked mortified as Penny continued to complain about the room, before they had even reached the top of the stairs. Justin pulled Jessica to one side. "Jessica, we have to arrange Mabel's funeral in the next few days. Get some rest and try and relax." Jessica just stood dumbfounded and seemed to be shaking on the spot. Justin looked in the direction that she was staring, it was then that he noticed a large rat staring back at them, nibbling on what appeared to be a chip. Suddenly the corridor filled with an ear piercing scream before Jessica fell backwards, fainting. Justin caught her as she fell back. He then picked his wife up and followed Anna and Penny up a flight of stairs. The door of their hotel room opened and, this time, Penny started crying. "We have to share a bathroom and sleep in the same room? This is the same bloody size as my walk-in wardrobe! This can't work. I demand to stay somewhere else!" she sobbed. Justin lay Jessica on the single bed and waited for her to come around. Jessica opened her eyes and instantly began sobbing and mouthed to her husband "I can't stay here" Anna saw this and addressed Justin "But nowhere else on the Island, all booked." Justin instructed Jessica to rest and meet him for lunch in an hour in the restaurant. He knew that her not eating properly was the reason she had fainted, as he closed the hotel door on Jessica and Penny leaving them to wail.

Frank and Agnes had enjoyed their taxi ride from the airport to the hotel. They had had their suitcases taken to their room by a very lovely porter. The room was beautifully decorated, with a balcony that overlooked the olive groves. After settling into their large room, they drank cold beers in the bar by the pool "This is the life, eh Frank?" Frank looked at

Agnes adoringly. "Yes petal, look you can get food and drink, twenty four hours. I can have a burger for my breakfast and my tea!" Agnes took a long swig of her beer "Eye, right posh and I saw it's eat as much as you like breakfast, lunch and dinner, and there is entertainment tonight! Karaoke!" It was then Frank spotted Carlos and Mrs May. "Hey up loves, come sit over ere, drinks are on me" letting out a cackle. Mrs May and Carlos joined them at the table, followed by Justin who, unlike Jessica, rather enjoyed the company of Frank and Agnes and was extremely fond of Mrs May and Carlos. Justin could not help but wince at the sight of Frank in a lime green thong that he was currently adjusting, loudly exclaiming "That's better that was chaffing". Agnes leaned forward on the table, her ample breasts straining against her red bikini top. "Nowt worse that chaffing, last year on holiday my thighs chaffed so much they looked like corned beef" she announced, causing Carlos to resist the urge to gag. He was also put out that the sheer bulk of Agnes obscured his view of Mrs May, who was looking rather fetching in a tasteful purple swimming dress.

A large group of ladies of various ages and sizes sat down on the table next to them, one was frantically trying to catch Justin's eye. Justin looked into his cocktail glass desperately trying to avoid eye contact. She was nearly fifty, by the look of her, and appeared to be casting her eye over any male under the age of forty. She stood up from her chair and said "Look at my tan" to Justin, lifting her dress up, revealing an impressive boob job. Justin looked horrified and removed himself from the table, excusing himself for lunch "Oooh lunch!" squealed Agnes. Suddenly the restaurant doors opened and there was a mass stampede of feet, as guests from every direction raced to get through the door.

Jessica was waiting in reception for Justin, as he had instructed. She didn't enjoy conversation with him anymore and agreed with Penny that he was demanding and boring. Jessica knew Penny would not come down for lunch, as she was feeling queasy from what she described as the 'rancid smell of body odour that lingered on the stairway'. Jessica just assumed that was the food cooking. Standing alone in the reception area, Jessica looked around at the cheap furniture and wondered how many thong clad buttocks had plonked themselves on the seats. She felt quite brave standing on her own, as she was sure that the hotel was full of bandits awaiting to pilfer the first person they saw. Suddenly Jessica felt the floor shaking beneath her feet and briefly started to panic that it was the start of an Earthquake. The ground started shaking beneath her feet, as she heard the thunderous stampede approaching. She looked on in horror as a sea of Hawaiian shirts and bulging flesh, escaping from various forms of swimwear, scrambling towards the restaurant. Jessica stood back, terrified that she would be swept up by the sweating hoard. They piled into the restaurant launching themselves at the buffet.

Jessica then recognised the booming voice of Agnes "Frank, they have chips, love!" Jessica cringed. 'Chips in a Greek restaurant' she thought. She then saw Justin approaching her "I am not eating in there, Justin" Justin grabbed her hand "You bloody are" He then pulled Jessica into the restaurant. Jessica's world started spinning as her eyes fell on Frank stacking his plate up, with what looked to be hotdog sausages, pizza and chips "Bloody lovely" he said, slapping his lips. Justin grabbed her elbow and took her to the buffet. "Eat" he said. Jessica approached the buffet "Is there any Greek food?" Jessica's stomach rumbled. "Look, Greek salad, olive oil, and pitta" said Justin, who started loading his plate up with moussaka and chips. A grubby looking child tottered up to the chips then promptly threw itself on the floor screaming, red faced, fists clenched and small feet stamping "I want ice cream, now!" Jessica, in a rare moment of maternal instinct, approached the child "Fuck off!" screeched the toddler. The room seemed to go deadly silent, just as Jessica snatched up a cone, dumped on some vanilla ice cream and shouted "Now shut up, you little bastard" launching the ice cream at the child, causing droplets to land on the child's head, dripping down its face. "I hope you are lactose intolerant" The child glared at Jessica "I want chocolate". Jessica scowled at the kid, who was swooped up by what Jessica presumed was his young mother, who promptly grabbed him chocolate ice cream, whilst cooing at him adoringly. "Aww Romeo my precious boy, mummy loves you." The child seemed at this point to look at his mother from under his blond fringe and growl "Stinky arsed." Jessica expected the mother to reprimand the little brat, however her response was to look on at the little sod claiming "He is such a strong character".

Jessica turned towards the buffet, turning her nose up at the greasy sausages and piles of chips and filled her plate with salad. "Justin get me a cocktail." Anna appeared "I get it" Justin and Jessica sat at their table. "Screaming orgasm, what you need" said Anna, presenting a highly decorated cocktail, complete with cherry and umbrella. Jessica took a sip, her eyes seemed to light up, and she took bigger and bigger gulps until she drained the glass. Justin sat back in amazement as he saw something he had not seen before from Jessica in a long time, a genuine smile. Justin smiled back and then leaned forward, whilst Jessica sipped her second cocktail that the beaming Anna presented. Justin broached the subject of Aunt Mabel "Jessica, you and Mabel were very close at one time, do you not feel anything about her passing?" Jessica finished her cocktail in two gulps and Anna appeared with another. "Well, the circumstances are odd - she swallowed a poisoned dart and the mistress of Charlie fled the scene. It's all rather embarrassing and Daddy is livid about it all." Jessica shuffled in her seat as she recalled how Aunt Mabel used to antagonise Daddy by sending Labour party candidates to the Manor house. Jessica realised she did miss Mabel and wished she had spent more time with her. Jessica looked up from behind the orange umbrella on the cocktail "I heard stories about Mabel, I never thought they were true, when is the funeral?" Justin checked his phone "In two days". Jessica started picking at her salad, complaining about the amount of olive oil and the quality of the feta.

CHAPTER 6

Penny lay on the hard bed on the cheap white sheets, eyes closed, she tried to sleep to block out the whole horrific experience. She knew she shouldn't have trusted Jessica; this hotel and the people in it reminded her of the life she used to know before embarking on her career of hoodwinking rich men. Penny had spent her life using her looks to better herself - to get away from the life of crime and violence she was born into. From an early age Penny had survived, walking on the streets for hours in all weathers, looking for food in bins whilst her mother lay on the grotty sofa in their one-bedroom council flat in a heroin induced stupor. She was soon taken into the care of the state and grew up in a children's home, where she continued to survive each day at a time. It was only when she reached the age of twelve, she realised that using how she looked, and who she befriended, would benefit her financially. Various older men would happily spend money on her in return for her company. She soon learned the art of keeping them wanting more and paying to wait. Penny then left them, after rinsing them of their money.

Suddenly a very Northern voice filled the room "Hey up, I'm Des and I am fresh off the boards at Blackpool. Tonight is Karaoke!" Penny let out a large sigh, this was all she needed. Penny walked to the balcony and looked across to the crowded bar. A portly male, sporting a quiff and Teddy boy jacket, was shouting into the microphone "I'll start tonight's singing... Caught in a trap, Ladies and Gentlemen" The crowd cheered as Des thrust his pelvis like gyrating old hipster. The more he thrust his crotch, the louder he got. In fact, it was so loud that Ray Norman was sat in his grey suit, tapping his foot to the music - he heard every word! As the song went on, the thrusting got faster until it looked like Des was having trouble with his hip. He stopped singing and limped back to the karaoke machine. "Next up, we have Agnes and Frank singing I've got you babe" Penny's eyes fell on the rotund figure of Agnes and the skinny frame of Frank. Jen didn't know whether to laugh or cry as Agnes and Frank squawked into the microphone and the singing got louder and more and more out of key.

Justin had forced Jessica to sit and watch the entertainment, although she had put up little resistance after drinking numerous cocktails. Jessica watched Des the Entertainer with a mixture of amusement and shock - she had never seen anyone with a quiff at the front of their head and a duck's arse hairstyle at the back. His stomach bulged over his jeans and she was thankful the shirt and Teddy boy jacket covered him, although she wished the shirt was buttoned up. She took a big gulp of cocktail number ten, as Agnes and Frank - both dressed in matching blue shell suits - got up on the small stage. The music started and the crowd cheered apart, from Jen, who seemed to be crying with laughter. Suddenly the stray cats that had been scrounging scraps off the guests ran off in fright, as the dulcet tones of Agnes rang out. The sound of them singing could only be described as a flat sounding drone with intermittent screeching. The crowd laughed, cried and clapped as the Cato walling continued.

Justin was laughing so hard he had tears streaming down his face. Suddenly Jessica did something she had not done in a long time, she laughed, and she laughed so hard she felt she couldn't stop. Her stomach cramped with the laughter. The singing stopped and the crowd went silent. All apart from Jessica and Jen, who were screaming with laughter. The more Agnes gave Jen the evil eye, the more she laughed. Jen started a slow clap, that got louder the more people joined in. Suddenly Justin cringed as the woman who had tried to talk to him earlier got up to sing, staring right at him she began singing Big Spender. Jessica noticed her looking at Justin and suddenly felt jealously creeping up within her. Justin felt terror as the aging predator thrust her hips and shook her breasts in his direction.

Jessica scowled at her as the song finished and she left the stage. The evening ended and most guests moved to head off to bed.

A young couple sat at the bar "Jordan, you have a face like a slapped arse" said the skinny lad with a broken nose. "Fuck off Neil, why don't you carry on flirting with that old slapper!" said Jordan, downing another pint of lager and banging the glass down with her meaty arm. "Don't be stupid, I only spoke to her after you snogged that barman before we left" said Neil, looking over her shoulder at the pouting older predator. Jordan took a gulp of her refreshed pint "Fuck off, Neil that was because you shagged that slag from the Isle of Wight, this is meant to be our make or break holiday to get back together for the kids." Neil scratched his skinny chest. "Yeah, well drink up and bloody cheer up, we are on holiday, I don't want to be looking at your miserable face all night." Jordan downed her pint. The guests started returning to their rooms.

Jordan and Neil had been in a tempestuous relationship for six years. Arguments and infidelity had become an ongoing issue, with Neil believing that he was a hit with the ladies. Neil, it seemed, was interested in every other female on the planet apart from Jordan, causing his partner to feel insecure and hurt most of the time. The fact they had two children kept the couple together until recently, when after a long break in their relationship they decided to travel to Greece for a week for a make or break holiday. Jordan's mother was dutifully looking after their two children and hoping that this holiday would break the relationship as she was not keen on how Neil treated her daughter and dearly wished her daughter would see the light and leave Neil for good.

As Jessica stood up from the table, she felt the room moving and she swayed. Justin grabbed her arm to hold her up. Jessica laughed, whilst trying to put one foot in front of the other. "I will take you to your room" said Justin, escorting her around to pool towards the apartments. "Can I come to yours?" asked Jessica. "You are drunk, Jessica" he said, although Justin didn't understand why his wife was sharing a room with Penny in the first place. He dearly hoped that Jessica would move across to his room, once she had sobered up in the morning. His concern was that Penny was trying to ruin their marriage and trying to push Justin out. Justin lost his balance and fell backwards; Jessica fell on top of him. Their eyes met and, as they both felt an overwhelming urge to kiss, the moment was broken by a loud argument.

"YOU ARE A DIRTY BLOODY TWAT, SOD OFF I AM NOT PISSED." Jessica and Justin looked over a sun lounger, to see Jordan pouring her pint over Neil's head. "YOU STUPID BITCH, WHY DON'T YOU JUST SOD OFF" Jordan then stormed off towards the apartments screaming "ARSEHOLE" Jessica then recognised the voice of Penny "Be quiet, you drunken morons, I am trying to sleep!" Jordan looked up to Penny, who was standing on her balcony "FUCK OFF, YOU POSH TART, YOU HAVE A FACE LIKE A PUPPIES ARSEHOLE" Penny was filled with rage "AND YOU ARE A FAT, UNCOUTH UGLY MUNTER, NO WONDER YOUR RAT-FACED BOYFRIEND IS LOOKING AT THAT CRUMBLING OLD HAG INSTEAD OF YOU!" Jordan stood, mouth gaping open. "Neil, am I fat?" Neil shuffled his feet "Well..." Jordan gasped "You think I'm fat? Well fuck you Neil" she stormed off towards the apartments. Neil returned to the bar and ordered another pint "I'm going back to the room, Neil" Neil continued to sip his pint. "I'm really going, Neil" said Jordan "Yes I know, piss off" said Neil, rubbing his ratty chin. Jordan sloped off and peace fell over the hotel. Jen had watched the whole episode from her balcony, whilst sipping a glass of wine. 'Who needs a television' she thought, snorting into her wine glass. Jessica and Justin staggered off towards the apartments, romantic moment lost, as Jessica suddenly had the urge to vomit into a flowerpot. Justin saw her back to her room and a shocked Penny, who greeted her with annoyance. "What have you done to her - she looks like a common strumpet?" Penny asked Justin, whilst they both dragged her to the single bed. "She had fun, Penny, something you should try." Justin sniped at Penny "Oh I can have fun, Justin, why don't you try me?" Justin laughed "Penny,

I would rather be stuck in an examination with Dr Prevo probing me, than have anything to do with you". Penny stamped her foot, as Justin walked away to his room.

Three star with a touch of Caviar

CHAPTER 7

Mrs May and Carlos had enjoyed their evening. Carlos had taken Mrs May to a local tavern overlooking the sea and introduced her to local dishes. Although Mrs May enjoyed a good old pint and a pie, she had a fond liking for Ouzo and gyros. Nicely full and merry, they walked along the beach, back to the hotel. Walking into the hotel, Mrs May and Carlos were startled by an almighty screech "That's Penny, I'd recognise that wail anywhere" said Mrs May, walking towards Penny's apartment. "I will come and help" said Carlos, puffing his chest out, resembling a pigeon and twitching uncontrollably. Mrs May knocked the door, which was pulled open by a dishevelled looking Penny "She was sick" growled Penny. "Sick all over my Jimmy Choo's, the room stinks and she keeps on about orgasms!" Mrs May walked into the room to see Jessica sat up in bed, looking very much like the child from the film The Exorcist. She approached with caution, ducking as Jessica projectile vomited across the room. "Penny, you go and sleep in my room, I will take care of her tonight" Penny weighed up her options, sleeping in a room of vomit or sleeping in a bed where Mrs May slept, surrounded by dowdy clothes. "Are the sheets clean, Mrs May?" Carlos twitched with disappointment – he had hoped he would be able to share a romantic night with Mrs May. He sloped off to his own room alone, to have a good long 'think' about her. Mrs May carefully placed Jessica in the recovery position, ignoring her requests for an orgasm. She then began the long arduous task of cleaning the room up.

Penny let herself into Mrs May's room and the slight whiff of cheese hit her nostrils. She looked around the tidy room and noticed a Chanel dressing gown on the back of the bathroom door. 'How does Mrs May afford Chanel' thought Penny, who then spotted a Dior dress folded on her chair. On closer inspection it appeared that Mrs May had numerous designer items. She opened a drawer and found a scrapbook. Sitting on the bed with it, she was astounded to see that Mrs May was previously a body builder, until she had the unfortunate accident with the death of the spectator. Penny lay on the hard bed, wondering how much money Mrs May had and how she could get her hands on it.

The next morning Jessica awoke, not entirely knowing where she was. She felt the hard bed beneath her and felt a hammering in her head, as she sat up and saw the rump of Mrs May poking out from under the white sheet from the next bed. Jessica promptly felt the urge to vomit and ran out to the bathroom, followed by Mrs May, who held her hair back as

Jessica clung onto the toilet for dear life and threw up. "You need a special remedy" said Mrs May, leaving the room. She returned a few moments later with a glass filled with the most revolting mixture Jessica had ever seen. Mrs May handed Jessica the glass "Down it "she said. Jessica wrinkled her nose as, in one swift movement, Mrs May grabbed her nose and forced her to drink, whilst Jessica gagged and spluttered. "Have a shower and wash the puke out of your hair" Mrs May instructed. Jessica, pale and fragile, heaved herself away from the comfort and security of the toilet seat. She gingerly removed her soiled clothing and stepped into the shower, scrubbing the smell of vomit out of her hair and off of her skin.

Agnes and Frank stretched out in their luxury bed. Frank had got up in the early hours to put their towels on the sun loungers nearest the bar and then crept back into bed, snuggling into Agnes', who was making gurgling noises in her sleep. Frank, being a postman, loved the early morning. He believed the world was different in the early hours of the morning and relished the cool air and the quiet. He then enjoyed returning to bed and cuddling into the warm body of Agnes. A few hours later, Agnes woke herself up with a loud snore. "Morning" said Frank "I'm starving, what time does breakfast start?" Agnes wiped the sleep out of her eyes "bout eight luv, let's get up, shower and get some grub in us." They both got up and prepared for the day. "'Innit 'OT" said Agnes, fanning herself with her magazine she had brought with her. "Sweating cobbs" replied Frank. "Let's get in that shower "he said, chasing a squealing, naked Agnes into the bathroom and flicking her bottom with his towel.

Anna had started her shift at seven. She had laid the tables and watched Maria and Gregos, the chefs, frantically frying eggs and bacon, cooking the beans and taking the hot food to the buffet. Anna didn't understand the English's love for baked beans that she cooked by the vat. With everything laid out at the buffet and the tables prepared, she opened the restaurant door – standing back whilst the swarm of guests exploded into the dining room. She watched the guests piling their plates up with toast and eggs. Frank and Agnes immediately spotted the bacon and fried eggs and began piling their plates up, terrified that the food would run out, whilst Agnes excitedly reminded him "It is eat as much as you like!"

Ray Norman was at the front of the buffet, taking the eggs off the hotplate soon as they were replaced. "It's alright, Ray, you can come back for more" said Jen. "Can I Jen, I don't want to look like a pig and what if they run out?" Jen ushered Ray to a table, while he kept a keen eye on the breakfast buffet, just in case he missed out. Ray loved food. For Ray, one of the big joys in life was eating - he liked it almost as much as horse racing. He tried most of the time to combine both, by eating a large pie while watching the horse's race past. Ray saw Frank and gave him a wave - both men hailed morning greetings to each other across the busy restaurant whilst Agnes, it appeared, had not quite forgiven Jen for laughing at her singing the previous night and chose to ignore her.

Jordan sat alone in the corner with her beans on toast, sti1ll upset from the argument the previous night. She looked across at Neil, who was still filling his plate up at the buffet. She then noticed the aging predator, dressed in tiny shorts and a leopard print bikini top, walk into the buffet. Jordon clenched her fists as Neil brushed passed her and the predator gave him a wink. Neil gazed at the predator and then walked towards the table to join Jordan. "Dirty old cow" said Jordan. "Shut up, I can't help it if woman fancy me. I used to be a boxer, woman loved it" sighed Neil. Jordan narrowed her eyes. "Yeah, Flyweight" said Jordan, looking around the restaurant and spotting Penny at the buffet. "Look, that's the posh old twat that shouted at us last night." Neil looked over at the skinny frame of Penny, wearing a very expensive looking beach dress and large sunglasses. She appeared to be picking bits of fruit up carefully from the buffet and inspecting it before putting it in her bowl. Neil took a mouthful of breakfast, regarding her dark hair and face; he was sure he recognised her - she was just like the attractive girl all the boys fancied at the children's home he grew up in.

Penny had ventured out of Mrs May's room to the restaurant. She was repulsed as she saw people shovelling baked beans into their mouths, without pausing for breath. Penny walked to the buffet and gingerly picked up a bowl, which she filled with fruit and yoghurt, fearful someone would talk to her - or worse - touch her. She sat in the corner away from the slurping and chewing, hoping she was far enough away not be hit by any crumbs spraying out of that rancid old postman Frank's mouth. He was regaling the diners around him with snippets of the Korean war, whilst Agnes looked on with pride, chipping in with "Bloody hero, and still goes to work!" She then ranted on about the laziness of youth and "How they don't know they're born these days" enjoying an audience nodding and agreeing with her.

Mrs May escorted a delicate Jessica to the restaurant with Justin and she assisted Jessica to a chair, wiping it down first for her, whilst Justin prepared a plate of bacon and eggs and plonked it down in front of her. "I can't eat that!" said Jessica, wincing from the pain her words made in her head. "Eat! Now!" said Justin. Jessica cut and ate a tiny bit of bacon, it had been years since she had eaten bacon or fried eggs she instantly felt alive. "See my magic formula never fails" said Mrs

May "Thank you, Mrs May" she said, slowly eating her breakfast. Mrs May was struck my how small and childlike Jessica looked nibbling on her breakfast. "I must start preparations for Aunt Mabel's funeral" said Jessica, looking forlorn. Justin smiled affectionately at her "I have organised everything for you" Jessica squeezed Justin's hand. The romantic moment was spoiled as Penny sauntered over to the table. "Jessica, you do realise what you are eating, you will only cry when you get fatter, and alcohol last night! I am ashamed" She sneered at Jessica. Justin could not sit back and watch Penny corrupt his wife any longer and stood up, causing his chair to clatter down behind him. "Penny, you bloody leech why don't you piss off." Suddenly there were a chorus of shouts, the loudest being Jordan "YOU SAGGY, OLD, UGLY BITCH, PISS OFF" Agnes got up, cheering "Go on, you tell that stuck up cow what you think of her." Penny stood her ground. "Oh look, the fatties are piping up. Chunky want a banana?" Neil took a longer look at her and suddenly he knew who she was. They had grown up in the same care home! He never forgot a face, or in Penny's case, a breast. That was Penny Smith. All the boys were rumoured to have had a go on Penny 'the bike' Smith. Neil was a lot younger than her but remembered sneaking into a cupboard with the older boys, who had all given their lunch money to Penny to watch her remove her clothes.

Penny left the restaurant followed by boos and made her way to a sun lounger, throwing the towel placed on it on the floor. She removed her sundress and lay back in her bikini. Her funds were running low and her cover story in the village was about to be exposed, as her sugar daddy wanted her out of his house after finding out about her affair with the plumber. She had told Jessica that Bert was her husband - he was an old pervert who enjoyed her dressing up as a dominatrix, whilst he wore a red PVC cat suit. She found him convenient, as she could tie him up or leave him in boxes for hours and she didn't have to have sex with him, as he hadn't been able to get it up for years after his spell in prison.

Bert had been caught by police during a sex game that went drastically wrong. He had hired a prostitute to dress up as a schoolgirl. The plan was to meet in a remote location and the unknown prostitute would be pulled into the car for a staged kidnap. He had stuffed rope, gaffer tape, lube and a ball gag into the boot of his car. He had also thrown a kitchen knife in for a bit of extra drama. He had waited at the spot and then saw a young schoolgirl walk along the lone country lane that went past his car; what Bert had failed to realise was that the remote location was being used that day for the local Catholic girl's school picnic. In his excitement he didn't notice that the girl was very young looking. As he ran after her in his balaclava, the girl screamed her lungs out. Bert was getting out of puff - the plan was she didn't run too far from the car, as Bert's trousers would be undone, ready for the post kidnap sex. Bert had followed the schoolgirl and chased her back to the picnic area where a number of young girls and nuns started screaming. "It's not what you think" said Bert, feeling the warm summer air on the tip of his exposed penis, where his trousers had fallen down. Sister Grace crossed herself and frantically began hitting him with her rosary, whilst another nun called the police. Within seconds police response cars surrounded Bert, whilst several crying schoolgirls were led away by specially trained officers.

However, much Bert tried to explain to DC Preek that it was a pre-arranged sex game, the more trouble he seemed to get in, as he was bundled into the back of a police car, protesting his innocence. He was then led into the custody centre, where a stern looking custody sergeant looked at him in disgust and he was led away to the cells. After eating a pot noodle and pasty, he was eventually taken into an interview room for questioning with a stern looking DC Everstar and Inspector Gill. His solicitor advised him to reserve his right to silence but Burt could not help himself and told the full story of his arrangement of the sex game. The detectives would not believe he was waiting for a prostitute. A stern looking DC Everstar asked him to explain the "rape kit" that had been found in the boot of his car. To which he tried to explain he had got the idea watching a film entitled "Schlong Blade." Bert was considered a danger to the public and remanded in custody, while the prostitute he had hired online - and he had paid two grand to in advance – had never had any intention of turning up to be kidnapped by an aging old pervert. She was happily using his money for a well-deserved spa day.

Although Bert didn't realise it, Penny was the canny prostitute living it up in the spa. Determined to make as much money as she could from Bert, she started writing letters to him in prison, after locating him on a lonely prisoner pen pal's website. Bert wrote in his letters about how "Big Ron" was waiting for him naked in his bunk most nights. Although Bert would not have objected to a bit of nooky with Big Ron, he had the embarrassing issue of not being able to rise to the occasion, since the rosary had smacked him hard on the penis and he kept having flashbacks to the Catholic school girls screaming and pointing as his exposed penis. Bert hoped his tackle would fully work again one day and spent many a night bunked up with a very disappointed Big Ron, listening to the shuffles of bedclothes and snorting way into the night. Penny, after weeks of writing to Bert and sending him a few curly hairs she found in her soap, gained his trust and was granted a visitor pass. Bert waited in the visitor room, a quiver of excitement running through him as Penny approached his table and, as promised, exposed her knicker-less undercarriage to Bert under the table. Bert soon looked forward to these visits and her cheeky downstairs winks, until one day a guard caught her legs akimbo, exposing herself to the inmate. The guard had caused a scene, shouting "Put it away, I am not having you stink the place out with that dirty rat" and dragged Penny out amidst cheers and wolf whistles from inmates. Bert realised at that point Penny was a keeper and allowed her access to his substantial property and gave her a generous allowance.

Three star with a touch of Caviar

CHAPTER 8

Penny felt initially that she had a winning card with Jessica inheriting the hotel, but now she was stuck here in this dump, with Justin getting his claws into her meal ticket. She had spent months bullying Jessica and lowering her confidence so she could take over her life. Every time she tried to approach Mrs May, she scuttled off or was in the company of that annoying, twitching driver of Jessica's. Drastic action needed to be taken so she could save her champagne lifestyle. She stretched out on the sun lounger, determined to at least get a tan while staying in this dump. She sat bolt upright with a start to see Agnes looming over her. "That's our Franks sunbed, you thieving bitch. He got up right early this morning to put towels 'ont loungers, limping down here he was with his war wound and here you are stretched out like lady bloody muck" Penny looked over her sunglasses at Agnes "Have you quite finished, you old trout!" Penny retorted, determined to show she was not going to be bullied by the daft old bat. Agnes then started cracking her knuckles and gave Penny a look that sent chills through her. Although generally Penny felt she could hold her own, she knew types like Agnes and knew if she pushed it too far she would end up with a black eye. Although Penny didn't associate with the villagers of Leighlands she was aware of

Agnes's reputation and heard a rumour that Agnes threw punches akin to Mike Tyson at the milkman, after he accused her of not paying her bill. Penny got up and sauntered off towards the bar, she could not be bothered to argue she had far bigger fish to fry.

Jessica had called Mummy and was surprised to hear that she would like to come to the hotel and attend the funeral with Ahmed and Mounir. Mummy had always enjoyed the company of Mabel and loved how she stood up to Daddy's misogynistic ways. Jessica arranged to hire a minibus for Carlos to take Jessica and Justin off to the airport. They had arranged to meet Mummy, Ahmed and Mounir from the plane and take them to the hotel. Jessica had spent the whole journey fretting that Daddy would arrive at the hotel with his newly acquired wife and battle lines would be drawn between the two families. Mummy and Daddy had avoided each other since their divorce, which had been a relief for Jessica, who previously was pulled between the pair of them and felt forced to take sides in all their arguments.

They arrived at the airport and entered arrivals, where Jessica spotted Mummy, who waved enthusiastically, while holding the hand of thirteen year old Mounir. He was pulling away from her, face red with embarrassment, while his Mummy shouted "Don't let go of my handy pandy, my little soldier."

Mounir scowled at her "I am thirteen years old, you are so embarrassing" Ahmed was beaming behind them. Ahmed adored Mummy and fell in love with her from the moment he set eyes on her. He had tried to advise Mummy to let Mounir become a little more independent, but to Mummy, Mounir would always be her baby and she fiercely protected him and never wanted him to grow up.

Jessica and Justin embraced Mummy and Ahmed in turn, whilst Mounir scuffed his feet looking at the floor. Mounir desperately wanted to grow up, but Mother just wouldn't let him. He had tried to tell her he wouldn't get a chill if there was a slight draft and he didn't need to hold her hand crossing the road. He did, of course, use his mother's overprotective nature to his advantage but it was a double cross to bear as, although he always got what he wanted, he never got the one thing he needed - freedom. Mounir knew his dad had tried on several occasions to give him some responsibility but he would never fully stand up to his mother. Mounir was miserable and caught in the dilemma of teenage angst.

They all set off with Carlos driving the minibus "Right let's get to the hotel. There is something I haven't had a chance to mention - Daddy might turn up with Zafia" Jessica said breathlessly. The group fell into silence "Isn't that one that looks like Toad from Toad Hall that you hate, mother?" Mounir grinned. "I was married to him a long time ago, he was rather a difficult man" said Mummy. "He treated you like a slave, the man has no respect for women, how did he find a new wife?" growled Ahmed. "Ordered her online after all the other potential wives left. Remember Maria, who completely lost the plot and set light to his newspaper at exactly eight o'clock in front of him and had to be restrained and sectioned?" said Jessica. "What about the one that got so drunk at a dinner party she started talking about the Labour party. Daddy threw her out of the house bodily" Mummy said laughing. Jessica was relieved that the prospect of Daddy showing up at the hotel appeared to not cause any anguish to Mummy and silently prayed it would stay that way.

They arrived at the hotel and Jessica arranged for Anna to show then to their rooms "I get my own room" said Mounir grinning from ear to ear. "Hold on" said Mummy, walking into his room "I want to ensure its safe. Don't go out on the balcony alone and don't leave the room without us. Do you have Teddy if you get scared on your own in the dark?" Mounir's face turned to thunder. "Leave me alone, Mother, I am not a baby" Mummy grabbed his face with both hands. "It's only because Mummy wummy loves her baaaby" Mounir shoved her off and slammed the door closed. "Bless him" said Mummy, giggling "Mounir, meet us by the stairs in ten minutes so we can go and play in the pool" she shouted through the door, before entering her room that was just next door. Justin looked at Jessica wide-eyed "I never saw her when I was a child, my parents were upset I wasn't a boy so I never got the over protection treatment" said Jessica, who felt deep sympathy for Mounir.

CHAPTER 9

Jessica heard a loud voice echoing through the reception area that could only belong to Daddy. "What's a man doing on reception, that's not how it is. A man who has travelled a long way wants to come into a hotel and see a nice pretty girl behind the desk." Jessica, along with a few startled guest's regarded the portly form of Daddy dressed like the man from Del Monte and gave a little inner cry. "Zophia, have you got the cases?" What appeared to be the spitting image of Cindy Crawford, wearing high heels and a tight red dress, tottered into the reception area, pulling in two large suitcases. "Here" she said, in a strong Polish accent. Jessica's receptionist, Paol, looked truly gobsmacked as Daddy leaned forward, asking him if he liked ladies or if it was a Greek thing to do woman's work. Paol stuttered that men work behind reception desks just as much a women. Zophia then continued to drag the cases away, after being pointed in the direction of their room. Daddy tittered to himself and looked around at the reception area, thinking it was very 'Mabel' - what with all the old furniture and pictures of stern looking women on the walls.

It had been a long time since Daddy had been on a trip, especially abroad. He was convinced he had seen most of the world and didn't really like it. He much preferred getting his English newspapers and keeping up with the horseracing, whilst enjoying a glass of port. Daddy, however, had previously had many mistresses from all over the world and was au fait with international cuisine. It was at that point his tummy gave a rumble and he sniffed the air and smelt what he was sure was chips. Daddy wasn't adverse to chips, he had had many a mistress who had made feasts including triple cooked chips. Daddy followed his nose to the restaurant and saw what appeared to be a hoard filling their plates up at the buffet, which consisted of chips and baked beans. He sat at a table, ready to be served and was promptly ignored by the passing waitress. "I say! What about some service?" implored Daddy, whilst frantically trying to catch the waitress's eye. The waitress gave him a withering look. "Go up and serve yourself to chips like everyone else." Daddy was shocked that a female had spoken to him that way and banged his fist on the table. "I bally well want service now!" The holiday makers looked at him in astonishment. "Pal, you go up and get your own grub" shouted one of the guests, who appeared to be peeking over a large burger at him. Daddy was shocked to see that the man who shouted was both topless and wearing shorts. Daddy always wore trousers and would only ever not wear a tie or cravat unless he wanted to sport a casual look! His stomach rumbled again, so he slowly approached the buffet and picked up a plate. Just like Mabel, he thought, making a man feed himself! Daddy spotted what looked to be some sort of pie and placed it on his plate, along with chips and slowly returned to his table. 'This was worse than going to war', he thought. He had never had to serve himself or eat greasy chips, even in Vietnam!

Daddy finished eating and was determined to have a word with Jessica about the self- service lark. It just wasn't cricket! He needed a stiff drink - and fast - to get over the experience. Daddy looked around, spotted the bar and sat at a free table nearby. "I say, gin and tonic here please." A large woman standing at the bar turned around and glared at him. "Wait your bloody turn!" Daddy removed his panama hat and took in the scene around him, not quite believing that a woman had answered him back yet again! What sort of a place was this? Daddy looked around him and saw a number of women spilling out of their swimwear – and not in a pleasant 'please your man way' but in an overweight hairy feminist way! Daddy blamed feminists for making women think they could be like men and stay just as hairy, judging by the woman who just walked past, with what looked like a haystack coming out either side of her bikini bottoms. Daddy was frantically looking around and wondering why he had not been handed his drink yet.

'Things are a bit shabby around here' he thought. Jessica eventually came out of hiding and approached Daddy at his table. He was still asking for a gin and tonic and being completely ignored by the bar staff. Jessica ordered two gin and tonics and sat across from him. "How lovely to see you, Daddy. I wasn't expecting you." Daddy looked stern "I have not only come to guide you through this hotel silliness, but for Mabel's funeral". Jessica hoped her fixed grin would make Daddy believe she was happy to see him. Daddy rambled on for what seemed hours about running a hotel and how it just wasn't practical for a woman to do it; the awful experience of having to get his own fodder and drinks, and the cheek of the women.

Jessica listened, unable to interrupt. Daddy hated women who interrupted, and she knew he would be disgusted if she dared. Eventually there was a slight pause in the conversation and Jessica advised him that Mummy, Ahmed and Mounir were staying at the hotel too. Daddy adjusted his tie and just said "Oh". Jessica's voice raised an octave, as she advised that Mummy also knew Mabel very well and had wanted to come to the funeral. Daddy then became pensive and looked into his drink, before stating "Your mother became very spoilt and forgot her place. She ran off and left me to fend for myself with nothing but a note! I had to take drastic action and find a replacement immediately!" It was then that Zofia walked into the bar area, turning heads as she entered, looking like a well-groomed thoroughbred. Daddy pointed her in the direction of the bar and Zophia automatically ordered Daddy another drink. She caught sight of Jessica and engulfed her in a hug, kissing both of her cheeks, "Darling, I am so happy to see you, you look so thin! And your eyebrows are amazing!" Jessica was flattered by Zophia noticing her eyebrows. Jessica had been through hours of torture, being plucked and threatened to get the perfect shape and was worried about the result, as Penny had told her she looked like a werewolf. Jessica observed how nice Zophia's brows were and hugged her back warmly.

The day of the funeral arrived, and Jessica awoke early. She was pleased that she had stopped sharing a room with Penny, who really didn't appear to care that she was leaving, but still managed to warn her that Justin would notice that she hadn't had a proper lip wax since she arrived. Jessica left the room in a blind panic, covering her top lip and had sent Mrs May out to find the best salon in the island to give her a tip to toe pamper and wax. However, Justin didn't appear to notice and had snored in her ear all night. At one time this would have annoyed her, but at the moment it was the comfort she desperately needed. Jessica slid out of bed and reflected on Mabel's hotel. To her, it still felt like Mabel's pride and joy and she was starting to see why Mabel had loved it so much. The staff were lovely and keen to help; the guests were quirky but all enjoying themselves and the hotel was comfortable and clean.

Jessica arrived at the church in a black limousine, dressed in a black trouser suit, arm in arm with Justin. She looked around at the mourners, who mostly wore sunglasses and had the distinct look of Mafia about them. Mummy, also dressed all in black, held tightly onto Mounir's hand, while he scowled at the other mourners. Daddy lingered at the back of the church, watching Mummy, who had changed since he last saw her. She had gained a little weight and was clutching onto that annoying scowling little brat, who was kicking the pew. Daddy reflected that Mummy used to make the most wonderful pate. He really missed that pate.

The church fell into silence as the doors opened and Reverend Meek staggered down the aisle, stinking of whiskey, grabbing desperately onto the ends of pews as he led the way for the coffin and pallbearers to the altar. Penny had decided to go along to the funeral -not that she knew Mabel or cared – she was busy scouring the mourners, looking for a man who could save her from her current financial crisis. She tried desperately to look sad, to gain some attention from the males around her, who seemed completely un-interested.

Suddenly a loud groan filled the church, causing all eyes to land on the unmissable figure of Reverend Meek, who staggered backwards into the choir, who retaliated by shoving him forward. Two small choir boys were forced to stand either side of him in the pulpit, holding him up, their cherub-like faces filling with terror as it dawned on them, he may fall on them. The congregation looked on open mouthed as Meek slurred out a sermon and memories of Mabel. He described her charitable nature as being like Robin Hood, as she merrily stole from the rich and gave some of her fortune to the local cats and dogs home. It was well known that Mabel despised most people and especially, men and children. This stemmed from when Mabel was asked to make an appearance at the local primary school for disadvantaged children and got shot on the bottom by a dishevelled looking lad of about ten. She retaliated by cuffing the boy around the ear and calling him a "snivelling bastard." She was escorted off the premises by Officer Carras, while she kicked and screamed, shouting that she would 'get the little shit'. Daddy growled, thinking of his last remaining memory, which was her punching him on the nose and driving off on her motorbike like a bat out of hell, giving him the finger.

The congregation stood to sing 'Morning Has Broken', while Reverend Meek led the pallbearers out to the graveyard on wobbling legs. They stood at the open grave, each throwing a handful of soil down onto the lowered coffin. Meek was reading from the bible "Ashes to ashes and dust to...AGGGGGGGGHHH!" Suddenly Meek lost his footing and stumbled forward into the open grave, arms waving like a flapping bird as he fell face forward, landing on top of the coffin with a loud 'thump'. There was a stunned silence from the mourners, as Meek floundered around and let out a loud scream of "Ouch!" A sound that could only be compared to thunder rocked the graveyard, as he let out a rip-roaring fart. Mounir let out a loud snort and started laughing uncontrollably. Mummy made excuses, claiming it was nerves or hysteria. Jessica was appalled by the massive, echoing rumble that had erupted from Meeks large rump and stood open mouthed, looking around the other mourners, who all appeared to be in a state of hysteria.

Jessica bravely peeked into the grave. "Is he dead?" she asked, as she looked down at the slumped body of the Reverend. With that, he let out a loud snore. Her face paled, as she looked down on the sleeping, snoring Meek suspended on top of the coffin, covered in dirt. Justin looked down into the grave as well - although he wasn't completely surprised by Meek's performance and hadn't known Mabel well, he was sure she would have approved of his antics and that is why she had left strict instructions that Meek must conduct her funeral.

Daddy was not surprised by the performance and believed it was just the kind of show Mabel would want to spite him and take away any dignity from her death. He was getting more and more fed up of woman wanting to be loud and trying to steal the show. He had watched a programme called 'Loose Women' recently, believing it to be a programme design to appeal to men. He had not thought about that sort of programme being on during the day and just assumed it was for men to enjoy in their lunch hours and time off! Daddy was extremely disappointed that the unattractive woman presenting it all stayed fully clothed and had the audacity to talk about current affairs and politics! It had caused Daddy to get his afternoon port an hour early, just to calm himself down. 'Women, who do they think they are?' He thought.

The crowd stood around the grave still, unsure what to do. Suddenly, a loud howling noise came from the grave. The crowd stood back, dumbfounded, as they witnessed the unforgettable bulk of Meek trying to scrabble out of the grave, hands clawing the soil in a panic and the flood of swearwords muffled by the soil. Jessica could make no further comment as Justin led her away. The mourners looked on and then dispersed. Daddy and Mummy eyed each other across the grave and nodded curtly at each other. The congregation started to disperse, leaving Reverend Meek in the capable hands of the recently arrived paramedics and fire brigade, as he was dragged out of the grave covered in soil, with the strands of his comb-over flying up in the air, looking like a wild banshee.

CHAPTER 10

Anna had spent the morning preparing the function room for the wake. Sandwiches and nibbles, chips and baked beans, all sat on the table, ready to please the English palate. The mourners piled in, quickly filling up their plates and starting to drink the local wine and spirits. Daddy stood by the bar, clutchinga large brandy, with Zophia, who he sent off to get him some nibbles. Mummy cringed when she heard the dulcet tones of Daddy "What the bloody hell is going on? Why are you here, woman, with your fancy man and kiddie?" Mummy looked Daddy up and down with disdain. "He is *not* my fancy man, he is my husband and a damn good one at that. We also have an adorable little boy" Mounir sauntered up, looking sulky. "Oh God, you were married to him? Mum, he looks like an old Boris Johnson." Mummy laughed and added "He's also a pompous old windbag!" Daddy turned pale. "You're a bloody leftie now too? Well, good riddance, you philandering, bra burning feminist!" Ahmed stepped forward, in an attempt to greet Daddy. However, Daddy decided to stomp off, muttering about pate, taking long march-like strides. Ahmed was still confused after his encounter with the old man - what was he babbling about, he wondered, as he watched the old field marshal stomp away, with his nose in the air.

Penny crept up behind Mrs May, who was busy chatting to Carlos. Penny gave her a big smile, "How lovely to see you. Thank you for letting me sleep in your room the other night. You are indeed a woman of taste." Mrs May was not one for smarm and gave a curt "You're welcome" and turned away. She knew that Penny would just be itching to get her hands on her carefully saved fortune. Penny didn't like being ignored, especially by the likes of a jumped-up housekeeper, however much Chanel she owned. Penny was just about to tell Mrs May what she thought of her, when she noticed an older male standing alone at the bar. She watched as a sudden breeze entered the room, lifting the front of his toupee. He asked for a drink at the bar and paid with a big wad of cash out of his pocket. 'My saviour' thought Penny, slowly edging towards him. Bad wig or not, she needed the cash.

Justin had tried to hold the hysterics in all afternoon. Reverend Meek had certainly given Mabel a send-off that would never be forgotten and Jessica was slowly recovering from the shock of seeing Meek clawing himself out of the grave, assisted by the paramedics, who assured her it was not the first time this had happened especially where the holy man was concerned. Jessica waited for all the mourners to leave the wake. She was truly surprised that every single one of the mourners had sidled up to her to ask her about the will, before promptly shoving fistfuls of sandwiches and chips in their mouths, only stopping when Reverend Meek entered shouting "Where's the craic?" and staggered towards the bar. Jessica was appalled by the antics of the randy old vicar, as he patted Zophia's bottom when he passed her and winked at Beata, who was working behind the bar. Beata was used to Meek chatting her up every night. She, as usual, swished her sleek blond hair over her shoulders and observed him through her long lashes. She felt sorry for Meek, as she believed that he had no family and had been cast out of Ireland after some sort of disciplinary hearing from the church. Meek had fled Ireland after he had been 'assisting' a young couple with their fertility problems and had been caught by the woman's husband, while he was hiding in their bedroom wardrobe after one such 'fertility session'. He has been chased out of the house in only his dog collar, much to the dismay of the local curtain twitchers and Neighbourhood Watch who promptly called the Garda. The sheer humiliation of the incident had caused Meek to start a new life in Zante, where he was able to behave just the way he wanted.

Jessica heard Meek start telling Beata about what nuns keep warm under their habits. "How disgusting, and a vicar too" she said to Justin, who stifled a naughty laugh. Jessica's attention was then drawn to Penny, who was talking to old Reginald. Why an earth would Penny be talking to him? Mabel had always said she had great respect for him as he liked the vagrant life and she liked the information that he would give her about rival poker gangs, who had no concerns about talking in front of a homeless man. He had indeed certainly cleaned up since his arrival the previous day, where he reeked so badly Carlos had had to manhandle him, stripping him and pushing him in the shower. Wails had emitted from the apartment, along with cries of "Get off me! I know what you Greeks are like and I am not going to be scrubbed there!" While Carlos scrubbed what he originally thought was a tan off Reginald's old rancid body, that horrifically turned out to be years of grime. He was given false teeth, as his own had decayed to nothing. His toupee had been washed three times but still had a whiff of old pee and sweat.

Officer Carras arrived at the hotel. He knew it was the day of the funeral but had to give Jessica some important news. He approached Jessica. "Sorry for your loss. I'm sorry but I have to leave to go to the hospital - an old lady has been mugged and I need to get to intensive care." Jessica looked saddened. "I am so sorry to hear that." Carras advised her that the lady was staying at the hotel with her husband, who was a war hero "Oh no, poor Agnes!" exclaimed Jessica.

CHAPTER 11

The word buzzed around the about the hotel that poor Agnes had been mugged and was in intensive care. Mummy watched Mounir's every move, in case there was a mad mugger on the loose. The guests at the hotel started a 'Go Fund Me' page and the afternoon was solemn. Children made get well cards for Agnes and the Go Fund Me page raised two hundred euros very quickly. Ray Norman had decided to purchase some flowers for the unfortunate lady and was escorted by Jen to the flower shop. Jen loved the smell of the fresh flowers and gazed gleefully upon the beautiful floral displays, while she waited outside for Ray in the glorious sunshine, sipping a cold glass of wine in the neighbouring taverna. She enjoyed the feeling of the sun kissing her skin and was shocked that such a crime had occurred in such a beautiful place. After twenty minutes, Ray came out of the shop holding a postcard. "I couldn't see any flowers, fancy not selling flowers!" Jen initially thought Ray was joking, but saw he was looking serious. "But Ray, it's a florist, I can see flowers!" Ray looked across at the shop. "I didn't see them, Jen." Jen snorted into her wine and ordered Ray a beer.

She wondered if her friend would ever be able to walk into a shop and purchase what he needed.

Hours passed without news of Agnes, until Officer Carras returned to the hotel. "How is she?" asked Mrs May. Carras looked grave. "She will be back this afternoon" he said. "She has had a good sleep". A child ran to Carras with a get-well card. "Why do you want a criminal to get well?" The guests looked confused. "Criminal? Agnes is not a criminal!" asserted Mrs May. Daddy stepped forward, "A veteran's wife is not a criminal, officer, you should be ashamed! And comrade Frank is a bally hero!". Carras looked serious. "That's right it was self-defence, according to war hero, Frank." The crowd of guests looked confused as Carras explained that Agnes and Frank were walking in the main town, trying to find a chemist for Frank's indigestion tablets. The mugger had run up and grabbed Agnes' bag. Agnes had swiftly turned around, punched the criminal in the face and wrapped the strap of her handbag around his neck, choking him until he passed out. She had then proceeded to kick and punch him repeatedly while he was on the floor and that it was the mugger who was in intensive care. Agnes herself had been in a police cell all afternoon.

This had all happened outside the local taverna, who had called police to report a fight. Officer Carras had arrived to find Agnes astride a skinny looking local lad, throwing punches at him while the crowd from the Taverna cheered. The ambulance arrived and the young lad was taken straight to A&E with numerous broken bones and suffering from the aftereffects of strangulation. Carras had bundled Agnes and Frank into his patrol car for questioning, trying to restrain her while her arms were flying out like windmills. "Lucky for you I was injured 'int war or I'd have knocked you into next week!" shouted Frank, from the police car window. They arrived at the police station and walked to the front desk, where a sleepy sergeant cast a lazy eye over them. "what you do?" he said, in his strong Greek accent. H was surprised to see the older lady react by punching and kicking an imaginary assailant. She also seemed to be shouting out her actions in a loud voice, in an accent he didn't understand. The man with her was also gesturing and a shouting slowly in a strange accent. He turned to Carras. "English woofers? Mental health? Or both?" Carras sat down at his desk and took a long draw of his cigarette. "Insane English. She was mugged and beat the living shit out of the criminal, who is now in intensive care." The desk sergeant sat back in his chair. "Bloody English. Take a statement and get rid of them. I can't be arsed with the paperwork and can you **PLEASE GET HER TO STOP STOMPING!** She gets louder with every thump! "Agnes did suffer with heavy feet and tended to stomp more, the more agitated she got. Her steps echoed through the police station as she was escorted out.

Neil lay back on his sun lounger and his eyes were drawn to the ageing predator, who was lying topless two loungers down. He then heard the unmistakable footsteps of Jordan behind him. "Don't think I don't know what you are staring at. It looks like she has spaniel's ears hanging down there." Neil let out a long-suffering sigh. "It's not my fault she has her tits out!" Jordan glowered at him, while he continued. "Women find me attractive, I told you this. I can't help it." Neil was then distracted by the high-pitched laugh of Penny, who was walking along with an elderly male. The man appeared to have what looked like a flat gerbil on his head. 'Penny is at it again' he thought 'she was a right goer for the right price'. Neil watched them walk towards the apartments. Jordan sat on her lounger and contemplated removing her bikini top, but thought better of it as the predator preened herself by the pool. She had clearly had a boob job, judging by the look of the two beach balls stuck to her chest. Jordan hated it when Neil got his eye on someone. He would always hide his rat-like face behind his sunglasses and watch the strumpets jiggle. Neil was watching predator laughing hysterically with anyone who went near her. He needed to find a way of getting rid of Jordan for a short while, so he could get his hands on those jubblies.

Reginald opened the door to his apartment, allowing Penny to enter first. "Why don't you go to the bar and get us a bottle of vodka to loosen us up!" she said. Reginald almost ran out of the apartment, eager to please Penny. He had found a way into the back of the bar area where he could help himself to anything he wanted. Once he left, Penny began snooping around the room. It appeared Reginald had only unpacked his toupee, as there were no clothes she could check the labels on. 'There must be money' she thought, opening drawers, but they were empty. Reginald returned with the vodka, which she immediately started downing. She was hoping that the drink would be the only stiff thing she would have to swallow, as Reginald made himself comfortable on the bed.

Penny asked Reginald to tell her about himself. "Well, I live out of a suitcase really." Penny felt hopeful. "Oh you travel a lot?" Reginald nodded and knocked back more vodka. "You could say that" he said. Then came the awful moment Penny had been dreading - Reginald removed his shirt and trousers, wearing only his vest, y-fronts and socks. "It's been a while" he said. Penny downed another vodka. 'The things I have to do for cash' she thought. Penny switched off and visualised the wad of notes Reginald had been flashing about throughout the five minutes of fumbling and huffing and puffing from Reginald on top of her. The exertion caused his wig to fly off, hurtling backwards and landing on the corner of the television. He then got up and went to the bathroom. Penny downed another vodka, hoping she would not be sick from the smell of Old Spice and the body odour Reginald seemed to stink of. Jessica waited for him to come out of the bathroom. "So what would you like to buy me, or do I get a cash gift?" Reginald looked stunned. "Sorry love, I don't have any money. I told you, I live out of a suitcase but mostly on the street. I am only here for Mabel's funeral and money was left by Mabel for me to attend."

Jessica stood up, throwing the bed sheet around her. "You have a wad of cash, I saw it!" Reginald shook his head "No, that was my novelty wallet, it looks like notes but its material, look" he showed her the unique wallet. Jessica felt the anger rising in her, along with vomit. She had allowed this tramp to violate her. "You owe me!" she screamed. "Sorry love, I thought you liked me. I spent my last twenty euros on the vodka. I am all packed up to leave in a bit - I only stayed last night. Must say, it was nice to have a wash, as it had been a while. I nicked some Old Spice from the Chemist, along with pile cream and soap for a proper scrub. My bits really ponged in this heat!" Penny couldn't hold the vomit in any more. She ran into the bathroom and threw up violently into the toilet. Reginald took the opportunity to pick up Penny's handbag and have a rummage through. He found fifty euros, which he pocketed and left.

CHAPTER 12

Agnes and Frank returned to the hotel and headed straight for the bar. Guests gathered around them, while Agnes boomed out "Stupid bastard - got the fright of his life, didn't he, thieving git! Didn't know who he was messing with" she said, flexing her biceps. Frank piped up "If only I wasn't injured from the war, he would have two of us to deal with!" A young child looked up at Frank "How did you get injured in the war, Frank?" Frank shuffled, took a long sip of his pint and then muttered "Don't ever talk about it, son. You kids don't know ya born." Daddy piped up. "Comrade, we will fight them on the beaches! I never forget one of my men and I never forget the face of any of my heroes. I am sure I know your face." With that, Frank looked sheepish and limped up to the bar to order another pint. Predator came up to the bar and sucked on her cocktail straw, staring at Justin - who was taking a breather from the drama of the wake.

Rev Meek had been fallen backwards off a barstool and stayed on the floor asleep, while mourners stepped over him. He seemed to come back to life and open his eyes when a lady in a skirt stepped over him. Justin was relieved that predator had covered her breasts. He was fed up with seeing the inflated and badly created monsters that protruded from her otherwise sagging body, pouting and thrusting at anything that moved. Justin then spotted a dishevelled looking Penny staggering out of the apartments, wild eyed and as drunk as a skunk, clinging onto the sun loungers as she walked dangerously close to the pool. Guests shouted at her to be careful, as she lost her grip on the sun lounger and fell into the pool with a massive splash. Neil seized the opportunity to be a hero, belly-flopping into the pool, his skinny frame hitting the water as he made an exaggerated leap to rescue her. This only resulted in him swallowing a bucket of water, making him gurgle and splutter. Mrs May noticed the commotion from the bar and pulled off her dress in one swift motion, revealing a well-muscled and sculpted body. She e ran to the pool and in a perfect and graceful dive, swam to Penny and Neil, saving them both and pulling them back to the side off the pool, before Agnes pulled both of them out with her thickset arms. Reverend Meek had also joined the gathering crowd and was insisting on giving Penny mouth to mouth, straddling her small frame with his large body. He lowered his mouth, reeking of whiskey, overs hers and placed his hands on her breasts, making her scream and slap him around the face with her open palm. Meek's face appeared to wobble uncontrollably from the impact, before he let out a loud groan and passed out on top of her, crushing Penny under his bulk, leaving her whimpering beneath him.

Predator was desperately trying to revive Neil -who didn't appear to be unconscious - but she sat astride him, pumping away at his skinny chest, until Jordan charged over. She dragged predator off him in one yank, leaving Neil desperately trying to cover the flagpole in the front of his shorts. He had to resort to rolling over on his stomach. Jordan was being restrained by Agnes, screaming "You dirty old hag, I will get you, just wait!" Predator laughed, much to the anger of Jordan, who was trying to escape the vice like grip of Agnes, dragging her to the bar. Jessica, upon hearing the commotion, raced out to the pool, her fists clenched, screaming "What the bloody hell is going on?" Her eyes then fell on the large frame of Reverend Meek on top of a dishevelled, wet and livid Penny. Mrs May was stripped down to a thong and bra that, if she wasn't mistaken, was from Victoria's Secret and was being watched by a twitching Carlos and a screaming banshee, which was being restrained by Agnes. "Oh my god, it's an orgy!" she exclaimed, as she saw the rat faced skinny lad grinning at the predator, who was in the process of removing her bikini top. Penny let out a wail from beneath the mound of Meek, so Mrs May marched over and dragged the dribbling religious man off Penny, who gasped for breath and started babbling about tramps and vicars, in between intermittent screams. Jessica stood up and addressed the guests. "There will be some big changes around here". Mounir had been watching the whole event from his balcony, while Mummy desperately knocked at his door to tell him to come off the balcony at once. "There are muggers about, riff raff fighting and you might fall off!"

CHAPTER 13

The next morning Frank woke up early to put the towels on the sun loungers. He had two reasons for being up early - the first being his ritual of putting the towels out on the sun loungers and the second due to the scream that had come from the room where Ray was staying. Frank had knocked on Ray's door, only for it to be opened by him looking panic stricken. He told Frank he had been attacked in the shower by a giant lizard. Ray was extremely animated and Frank realised that in five minutes of conversation that the description of the lizard had grown in size and now appeared to be the size of a crocodile! Frank was ushered into the room to get rid of the beast, only to find a very small lizard looking back at him. Frank picked the poor thing up, bade Ray goodbye and walked down to the sun loungers with a spring in his limping step. He then released the lizard, laughing and muttering to himself about crazy characters. He stopped dead in his tracks when he saw a big sign that informed guests that no towels were to be placed on sun loungers before 08:00. He was further shocked to see a beefy looking security guard, standing with his arms folded, watching him carefully. Frank returned to his room, eager to tell Agnes, who thought it was a bloody cheek and said she would have a word with reception about it.

Anna looked around the tidy restaurant and felt quite excited at the prospect of table service. No longer would she be heaving heavy vats of beans to the buffet area and the chefs were excited about cooking fresh dishes to order. Jessica had started implementing her new ideas into the hotel. The new security guards had been patrolling the sunbeds overnight, to ensure guests didn't squabble over sun loungers and were currently a new shift of staff were preparing to keep order during the day. As breakfast time approached, a slight panic rose in Anna's stomach. She had spent years watching guests pile their plates up with bacon and eggs, shovelling great mouthfuls of chips into their dribbling mouths. Anna then saw an angry looking crowd at the reception desk, so she walked over, remembering her training of 'if they shout pretend you don't speak much English'. The crowd erupted into shouts of dismay over the new sun lounger policy, the loudest being Agnes, shouting "Not allowing a war hero to put towel down, he needs to be close to the bar with his limp!" Anna shouted over the crowd to try and make them hear her "It's a new policy from the manageress." Agnes screamed back "We don't bloody like it! I will be making a proper complaint about this". The crowd dispersed towards the restaurant and Anna wished she could hide under the desk as she heard "What the bloody hell is this, where's the buffet?" Anna approached the restaurant and, along with the other scared looking waiters, started showing bewildered guests to tables.

Frank and Agnes were handed menus, which they looked at with faces filled with disgust, "Full Greek breakfast, oooh no I don't like that foreign muck. You don't come on holiday for foreign muck!" Agnes slammed her meaty fist on the table. "Greek yoghurt and fruit? Where are the black pudding and beans?" This started an uproar in the restaurant, with a chorus of "We want a fry up, we want a fry up!" Anna shouted over the crowd. "Please read menu, full English there." Anna began taking orders for mostly full English breakfasts. Ray walked straight up to where the buffet had been the previous day. He seemed not to have noticed, or heard the complaints of the other guests. Jen ushered him back, informing him it was table service. "How can it be a buffet and a table service, Jen?" Anna came to the table to take their order. "I'd like breakfast" said Ray. "Certainly, which?" said Anna. "Breakfast" said Ray "with poached and fried eggs." Anna returned with a plate of fried and poached eggs. "Where's the sausages and bacon and toast?" Anna looked more confused, but returned to the kitchen with the further order.

Jordan was barely speaking to Neil after the poolside incident with the predator. "Fruit?" said Jordan. Neil put his menu down. "Well you keep saying you want to lose weight." Jordan felt full of rage as she glared over her menu at him. "Why are you such an arsehole?" Neil carried on looking at his menu. "You're in a good mood again!" He was completely disregarding Jordan's feelings and her heart felt heavy. Neil never made her feel nice, or wanted. His wandering eye filled her with heartbreak and insecurity. Whatever happened, or whatever she said, it would always turn around and be twisted to her fault. When things hurt and she addressed them with him, she was exaggerating, or it never happened. Jordan felt some days she was going mad and as she lost her grip on reality, the more isolated she felt from the rest of the world.

They ordered their full English breakfasts and turned to the loud shout from Agnes. "One sausage and a bit of bacon like in the bleedin war! Are we on rations?" The guests were presented their breakfasts, which were indeed slim pickings compared to the previous 'all you can eat' buffet. The kitchen was kept busy with triple orders of extra fried bread and bacon at *all* the tables. Jessica walked into the restaurant and Frank spotted her immediately. "Hey! What's all this, why no buffet breakfast? I didn't fight a war to be put back on rations." Jessica pulled herself up to her full height. "Ah Frank, I knew you would be pleased with the table service, it means no more limping up and down on that wounded leg of yours!" Frank and Agnes looked at her, open-mouthed "ere what about him having to limp half mile to bar, now we can't put our towels down." Jessica gave a big smile. "There will be a full cocktail service around the pool, no more limping about for you" Agnes seemed to deflate. Jessica had felt a surge of confidence since moving herself out of the room she shared with Penny and felt positive about the changes she was making to the hotel.

.

CHAPTER 14

Neil thought 'today is the day to get Jordan out of the way' and get his hands-on predator. He decided to get Jordan so drunk that she would need to lie down for the rest of the day. He had got up early, walked to the local mini mart and purchased a bottle of vodka while she slept. In preparation he had already laced her breakfast orange juice with it and she hadn't seemed to notice. He chose their sunbeds and laid her towel down for her, before offering to get her a drink. Jordan was shocked by Neil's change in attitude and hoped this was the reversal she had been waiting for. He returned with a very strong long island iced tea for her. "Come on Jordan, drink up, its hot today and we are on holiday!" Jordan kept drinking the heavily laced cocktails that Neil kept bringing her, until the world started to spin around. "I don't feel well" she said, as Neil led her off to their room, so she could rest. He waited for her to start snoring and went out to the pool.

A topless predator bounded over to him. "So, todays the day" she said in a husky voice. "How about I meet you in the pool toilets in two minutes?" She then headed off towards the grotty toilet block. 'No one will find out' he thought, as he watched predator walk off. After two minutes, he sauntered toward the toilets, the smell of urine hitting him as he walked in. 'Needs must when you want to get your end away', he thought. Neil watched as Predator pulled her bikini bottoms off; his eyes filling with lust as she pouted and thrust her breasts at him. 'Little Neil' stood up like a flagpole and soon they were indulging in frantic nookie. Poor Mr Lee in the next cubicle tried to block out the sound of the gasping and clapping of skin. Old Mavis, his wife, had never made noises like that and at one point he wondered if the woman was okay, as she was yelping and panting like a rabid old dog. Mr Lee made the decision to leave the toilets before they finished. He didn't want any rumours starting that he was involved in a ménage trois! Mavis would kill him, especially after she caught him eyeing up the old predator's topless form earlier in the week. He scurried out with a look of dismay on his face, loudly saying "They are at it in there!" Suddenly all eyes were on the toilet door, waiting to see who had bonking in the toilets.

Predator gave her final yelp and Neil sat back satisfied. He had another notch on his bedpost. Then his world fell apart.

"Just to let you know, I had a few lumps down there the other day. I am going to see the Doctor when I get home, but you should be fine." Neil gaped at her. "You mean, you might be infected with something?" Predator pouted at him and changed the subject. Neil wanted to escape and felt for the door handle. "So, when are you telling the fat one you came here with that you have moved on, or will I be doing that?" she asked. Neil looked blank. "Well, I assume we are an item now. I came here looking for love and here you are!" Neil sat on the toilet seat, his head in his hands. "Now hold on, I thought this was just a bit of fun and you didn't tell me you had lumps and things!" Predator screamed. "You used me, you bastard!" and started crying hysterically. This was not going to plan for Neil - at this rate, Jordan would find out what he had been up to. Oh God and the lads at home could never find out about this! He had spent months trying to big up his status, telling them how he used to be a boxer and how many fights he had been in; how women fell at his feet. This would ruin everything! He needed to fix things with Jordan, and fast, so he could convince her that Predator was some weird nut job, if anything was to come out.

Agnes was watching the pool toilet door, waiting for the lanky rat looking lad to come out. She knew he had been in there with that topless hussy, while his girlfriend was out of the way. It appeared everyone around the pool was also aware, as

Neil felt all eyes on him as he scurried back to his sun lounger, after downing a very large brandy. A few minutes later, a tearful Predator came out of the toilets and lay on her sun longer with a face like thunder. Agnes looked across at Frank, who was eating his usual after breakfast burger and gulping down a pint of beer. "I don't think that was a good jump. That hussy doesn't look happy at all. That ratty boy keeps downing brandy and is as white as a sheet." Frank put his pint down. "There is an art to pleasing a woman, Agnes. These youngsters just don't get it" He looked at his wife adoringly.

Penny delicately walked from her apartment to the pool. She decided today would be a day to recover from her horrific experience the day before and have some time off of man hunting - not that there were any men rich enough on this island to support her needs. Just as she lay down on a discreet sunbed, the lanky rat faced boy she had seen about the hotel approached her. "Alright Pen?" She looked up over her sunglasses at him. "I don't believe I know you and it is Penny to you." As he continued staring at her, Penny wondered if he had special needs. "You are Penny Smith, from Old Farthing's foster home, aren't you?" Penny sat bolt upright, her world was crumbling around her. She thought she had buried her past. "You have the wrong person" she said, dismissing him. "I don't. You are Penny 'the bike' Smith. All the boys hopped aboard.

You look like you have done alright for yourself, although I was surprised to see you with that bloke with the wig yesterday. Rumour has it, he's a tramp!" Penny glared over her sunglasses at him. She didn't want her reputation to be ruined and after the previous day, the thought of touching his skinny body filled her with repulsion.

"What do you want Neil?" He looked her in the eye. "Well, Pen, you look like you are doing alright for yourself and us being old friends, I thought maybe you could give me, say, a thousand euros to keep your reputation safe?" Penny sat bolt upright. "I will let you think about it overnight, Pen." He then walked off in a fast trot, ignoring the older topless predator, who was crying beneath large sunglasses. Penny then heard loud stage whispers from the next sun lounger, where that corse postman and his grubby wife sat. "Well, that ratty boy did the job with that topless trollop and high tailed it. Left her in tears. Look! He has gone back to his hotel room, back to his girlfriend, the cheeky sod." Penny sat back on her lounger. 'This could be fun' she thought, and it would keep that skinny creep from exposing me. She slowly walked towards Predator, who seemed to shrink as Penny loomed over her. "What's the matter?" asked Penny, feigning sympathy. Predator continued sobbing beneath her sunglasses. "Let's get some drinks "Penny said, walking to the bar, followed by a snivelling Predator. They sat in the corner of the bar with extra strong long island iced teas. "He has been all over me, all holiday and then we went to the toilets to be together and..." She began crying even more hysterically. "He used me! He had full on sex with me and when I told him that I had had a few lumps, he went all cold and he won't leave that fat girlfriend for me!" Penny held back the laughter, and her glee, as the information Predator was giving her sank in. "I came here for love and I thought he would leave that fat girlfriend and be with me, but he just kept on about lumps!" Predator took a big gulp of her drink. "We go home tomorrow, all on the same flight." Penny patted Predator's hand and then wiped it on her sarong. "He can't get away with this. Trust me, we can ensure that he never hurts people again. I mean, we need, to ensure that fat girlfriend is aware of what he has done to you." They clinked glasses, as they formed a plan between them.

Jessica had made real progress with her changes to the hotel. She had turned every lunchtime into a barbeque. This seemed to please all the guests, as they shoved gyros and kebabs into their mouths, being watched by the stray cats, who had long learned how to play them for food, weaving their way around the legs of those most likely to give up a piece of chicken or fish. Jessica had found that even Frank had little to complain about, since he had to do very little walking and realised he could still have three breakfasts if he wanted. Justin had been very attentive to her and had encouraged her in her hotel changes. She felt her confidence swell and a sense of pride, as she looked around the hotel. She had updated the furniture in the lounge and had big plans to modernise the bedrooms. For the first time in a long time, Jessica felt in control and realised just how much she loved Justin. Now Penny seemed to be staying away from her, she saw her old friend in a different light. Penny may have been a friend when she thought she needed her, but in reality, she had pushed everyone Jessica loved away, especially Justin. Jessica had lost her confidence, money and almost her marriage because of Penny and now felt very angry indeed.

Ray Norman had purchased a new pair of trousers before the holiday. He didn't want to try them on while in the shop and had placed them in his suitcase, thinking they would be perfect for Greece. He tried them on in his hotel room, to find that they were about four inches too big around the waist. Ray decided that he would find a tailor, so that the trousers would fit nicely on him. He approached reception, where Anna was busily tidying the desk. Ray explained that the trousers were four inches too big and he needed to find a tailor. Anna gave a broad smile and explained that her mother was able to assist, as she was a seamstress and could get the trousers repaired overnight for him. Ray was very pleased with this, as the trousers were very nice, and he had paid a lot of money for them. He trotted off to his room and returned with the garment for Anna, happy in the knowledge he would be able to wear his smart trousers on the last day of their holiday.

Mummy grabbed Mounir's hand, much to his disgust, and led him to the pool "Right, sun cream on please. We can't have my little prince getting burned. Oh and I have armbands for you." Mummy started blowing up the armbands. "I don't need them, I can swim, stop embarrassing me!" Mounir grumbled. "Well stay where I can see you and don't go in the deep end" shouted Mummy, as Mounir strode off towards the pool. Mummy watched his every movement, especially when she noticed that the ageing old hussy was whipping her bikini top off again. "Disgusting" she muttered, hoping that Mounir would not notice. Ahmed looked across at Mummy. He adored how eccentric she was and how, even though they had been married for over thirteen years, she still didn't know how much a loaf of bread cost. He decided he was a very lucky man. He then saw that Mummy's face was fixed in a frown. She had seen Mounir staring across at the woman by the pool- the one who always had her boobs out. 'Good on you, son' thought Ahmed, although he didn't dare mention to Mummy that he had noticed as well, as Mummy could get quite jealous. When Mummy got jealous and shouted, she would sound all posh. The last time Mummy had got jealous, was when a younger woman kept attending the village shop and partook in flirty banter with Ahmed, who was not interested in her in the slightest, but played along for the custom. Mummy had got angrier and angrier and refused to speak to Ahmed, until one day she exploded and, in a very posh voice, shouted that the woman was " The bally limit" and told her to "go away and boil her head!" The young woman left the shop sharpish, as Mummy hurled bread rolls at her and called her a "cheap hussy," much to the astonishment of Ahmed, who was very upset to have lost a customer.

Agnes and Frank walked to the bar. "ere Frank, look at Alan Whicker over there!" Frank giggled. "Yeah, looks like a right posh git. Said he was a Field Marshal or something." Agnes looked confused. "How does that work then? You mean like one of them blokes that wear an orange tabard in fields and direct traffic?" Frank explained it was a rank in the army. They sat on the table behind, as they saw Daddy sitting with his very young-looking wife. Agnes was desperately trying to earwig at what was being said, but every time one of them said something, Agnes was unable to hear due to Frank talking or coughing. Agnes nudged Frank and mouthed "Be quiet." Frank looked around him, in an exaggerated fashion "Why?" Agnes then whispered that she was trying to listen "Why are you whispering?" bellowed Frank. Agnes kicked him under the table. "Why are you kicking me, Agnes, what is it?" Daddy then turned around. "Ah comrade! How are you my good man?" Frank gave an awkward grin and said he was fine. Daddy then lamented on the Korean War, while Frank nodded. Agnes tried to change the subject. "'Ello love, nice sun dress you got on." Zophia beamed at her and thanked her. She liked ladies like Agnes, as they reminded her of the English television programmes she had watched in Poland, when she was a child. The shows where all the women had rollers and nets on their heads and would shout at their husbands. Zophia dearly wished she could shout at Daddy. When she first met Daddy, she thought that her life would be one of riches and sparkling dinner parties. She had ended up as a housekeeper, cleaning the Manor and picking up after her husband. She was relieved that Daddy was quite happy to spend his day's horse racing and shooting, and therefore she didn't have to spend a lot of time with him. Zophia loved the days when, knowing the house was tidy, all she had to do was give Daddy his paper in the morning and then she could settle down with a vodka and invite her friends over. She just needed to devise an escape plan, so she could run away from the misogynistic monster and take a large share of his cash with her.

CHAPTER 15

Neil decided that he needed to take drastic action to ensure Jordan didn't find out about the whole public toilet 'incident'. He knew that with most issues, he could talk Jordan around but if she actually thought that he had cheated on her on their 'make or break' holiday, he stood to lose everything. He started devising a plan so that Jordan would not be approached by that awful predator woman, or Penny. He knew Penny would enjoy ruining his life and wished he had not tried to antagonise her.

He decided the only way to keep Jordan on side was to charm her and be what she wanted - the perfect boyfriend. He could then probably convince Jordan that predator was crazy, jealous of Jordan and that it wasn't his fault women fancied him. Hopefully his girlfriend wouldn't believe it if Penny and predator started causing issues. He reflected to himself that it was Jordan's flat he lived in. She went to work while he claimed benefits and looked after the children - that is when he was not playing on the X-box! Jordan went to work every day as a Carer to support the household and found it a difficult and challenging job, but she kept at it. He returned to the hotel room to find Jordan reading a magazine. "How you feeling?" he asked. "Alright, after I was sick. I don't know how I got so pissed" Neil didn't think staying at the hotel for tonight's Greek dancing was going to be a safe option, what with predator and Penny likely to rock the boat. "Let's go to the McDonald's in town, get some free shots and walk along the beach tonight. Spend a bit of time together." Jordan nodded in amazement. "Yes Neil, I would like that." Neil then snuggled up to her and started pawing at her. 'Job done', he thought. He always knew how to twist her around his little finger.

Mrs May and Carlos had enjoyed their time in Greece so far, taking in the local scenery and Carlos had enjoyed introducing Mrs May to Greek food and traditions. He had even held her hand on the way back to the hotel the previous night. Mrs May had noticed Daddy and Zophia. "Oh God! It's that pompous old fart" said Carlos, who looked hard at Daddy. "He looks like a big full moon and who on earth is the mutton with him?" Mrs May filled Carlos in on how Mummy had left Daddy for a younger man, who ran a corner shop, and Daddy had decided to find an online bride, instead of hiring a housekeeper, believing it would save him some money. He was also convinced that women enjoyed housework. Zophia had come from a very small village in Poland, living in poverty and had believed coming to the UK and marrying a rich man would save her and her family, who she sent money to when Daddy allowed it. Zophia worked day and night, making him happy. "She must be a tough lady to cope with him and his needs" said Carlos, who knew how demanding Daddy could be. Daddy didn't believe that people from other countries should live in England but didn't seem to mind if it meant employing staff at minimum wage or marrying Polish brides. Daddy always seemed to be able to justify his double standards.

Mrs May was as pleased as punch to be promoted to Head of Security at the hotel and prided herself that, when the hotel bar closed at night, she would ensure all guests were where they should be. She would also make sure that the gates were locked and all, as Jessica described them, 'riff raff', were quiet when returning from the local's clubs on the nearby strip. The most difficult job was usually escorting Reverend Meek off the premises. Meek could usually be found passed out, stretched over the bar in various states off undress. Meek tended to be at his worst when he conducted christenings, due to the fact he disliked children and drank vast quantities to get through such an event. Today had been one of those days and had caused dismay and concern across the island. This morning he had consumed his body weight in Whiskey and was wobbling about over the font, with the wailing baby balanced precariously in his arms. Meek had lent forward slightly and dropped the screaming child in the font, while he instructed the infant to "in the name of god shut up!" The parents had snatched up their child and told Meek he was a disgrace, to which he responded "and your child has cloven hooves and a tail. He is the beast!"

The parents had left sobbing, while Meek shouted words of fire and brimstone at them. He had then staggered to the hotel, ranting about deliverance and wailing little bastards, and hauled himself up on his favourite barstool, much to the amusement of the other guests – most of whom had crowded into the bar to watch his antics. Meek, having such an audience, rose up from his barstool in a moment of madness and started shaking his Bible, shouting about demons and damnation, offering to out the demons via exorcism for any poor souls that needed his assistance. The watching crowed looked around at each other and started to edge away, until Meek spotted Penny walking into the bar. He grabbed her and Penny screamed and started trying to fight him off. "The power of Christ compels you, out demon!" His wannabe exorcism victim screamed, as Meek held her down. The noise alerted Jessica, who approached the bar accompanied by her new Head of Security and was flabbergasted to see Penny foaming at the mouth and screaming, while Meek splashed water in her face and instructed the crowd to hold her down, so he could rid the demon from her. Agnes had launched herself forward and was holding the wailing Penny down by her arms, with a menacing grin on her face. Frank held her kicking legs, as instructed by Agnes and Meek started shouting in tongues, as the guests circled around them, unsure if this was the entertainment for the day or a real exorcism.

Meek was ripping the crowd up into a frenzy, clapping and ordering the guests to shout "Out demon" while Penny writhed, swore and tried to claw at his face. Eventually, Penny passed out and Meek then managed to get the guests clapping and singing "Oh happy days" together, parading up and down shouting "Praise Jesus!" Jessica would have stopped the ridiculous display but, as it was Penny, an evil imp was nudging her to allow it to carry on. Jessica sat at the bar with a large cocktail, watching the scene unfold and feeling completely satisfied that Penny was the subject of such a display. Eventually, Penny was dragged away to her room by Mrs May, who lay her in bed and attempted to fan her. Penny awoke to Mrs May looming over her. "Am I dead?" she said, in a small voice. "No, you have just been exorcised." Penny then recalled the full horror of Meek's attempts to purge an evil spirit out of her and promptly passed out again.

Greek night was in full swing at the hotel -the guests sat in the restaurant and looked with confusion at the menu. "It's all foreign" said Frank. Agnes pointed at the menu "Look fish is on the menu!" Frank put his copy down. "Does it come with chips, like?" The waiter looked confused and asked "Instead of Greek potatoes?" Frank then also looked confused. "Fish always comes with chips, not foreign potatoes!" He then turned to Agnes. "There is tarantula on the menu, foreign muck and balaclava for pudding" Agnes face filled with disgust. "Foreign muck like mooooosaaaaakaaaa!" Frank took a big gulp of his beer. "They would do better to put a nice roast dinner on the menu, it is Sunday, you know." Agnes was very confused - Frank was right, it was Sunday and you *always* have Yorkshire pudding on a Sunday. A loud voice boomed across the room, that Agnes recognised as that posh git, Field marshal. "I will have one taramasalata, a gyros plate and baklava and Zophia will have the same. Oh, and a bottle of your finest red wine." Frank turned to Agnes. "That mad posh bastard is having tarantula, a gyro and balaclava, dirty bugger." The waiter was still hovering by Frank, looking stressed and worried. "Fish and chips for us and more beer, mate."

Illios hated waiting tables and wished the English had been left with their buffet. He didn't understand why the scrawny man and his big wife wanted fish with chips, as that was not on the menu. 'That was the thing about the English', he thought. 'Always difficult'. He was, however, pleased that he did not have to serve the loud man, who he had been was told was Jessica's father. No-one wanted to serve him. Illios took the fish and chip order to the kitchen and then waited for the shouting to start. Jessica had recently employed new chefs at the hotel and the improved kitchen ran like clockwork, but Head Chef Paul did not take kindly to menu changes. Illios passed the order to Paul, who spat out "Fish and stinking chips? What is this English rubbish? They get Greek fish and potatoes or they can piss off!" He then started shouting at his Sous Chef, who had overcooked a piece of halibut and threw it across the kitchen. Illios dearly wished Paul would go out into the dining room and explain the fish and chip situation, but knew he would refuse. Illios sloped off back to the restaurant and explained to the scrawny bloke and his wife that there were no chips to be had. "No bloody chips at all? Disgrace!" said the woman, while her husband tutted. Illios tried to calm the situation by saying how nice the potatoes were. "Bleedin' better be" said the woman, who Illios had heard had put a mugger in intensive care recently. He wasn't surprised by the look of her - he had seen wrestlers who looked like her on the television.

Predator had heard about the exorcism of Penny and decided to visit her in her hotel room. Mrs May had informed her that it had taken several slaps to stop the hysteria. Mrs May didn't mention she had rather enjoyed slapping the devious Penny around the chops and had found it rather hard to stop. Predator had sat on Penny's bed, much to Penny's disgust, and cooed how wonderful Penny was and what an awful experience she had been through. Although Penny didn't care much for the woman sitting in front of her, she knew she would be an easy target to use to get her revenge on Neil. Also, who knows, if things got too desperate, she might tolerate her enough to stay with her for a while, provided she wasn't too poor. Penny noted that predator had been able to afford a boob job, so she must have some money. Penny put on her brightest smile and agreed to go to the restaurant with her. They stood in the doorway of the restaurant and waited to be seated. Penny didn't like waiting, huffing and stomping her feet until, eventually, they were given a table. They both fell sllent while they read the menu. Penny glanced around at the other diners and looked down her nose at them when they caught her eye.

Jolene didn't know that most of the hotel had nicknamed her predator. She just believed that the dirty looks and insulting comments she got were due to jealousy, because of her fabulous boob job. She took great pride in her appearance and knew she looked good for her age. She had come to the island with her work friends, who were all nannies and had been deserted by them one by one, as they had all found themselves holiday romances. Jolene wanted to find love and from the moment Neil had arrived, he had been giving her the eye. She had jiggled, laughed and flicked her hair at him and he had responded nicely to all the flirtation. It was a thrill for Jolene to watch and wait for Neil's girlfriend to either go to bed, or storm off after an argument, so she could sidle up to him. Neil had told her that he was waiting for an excuse to finish with Jordan, but was worried about their children, which was the only thing that kept him with her. After one extreme argument with Jordan, where she had poured a pint of beer over his head, Neil had taken Jolene for a romantic walk along the beach and they had kissed. Neil had made promises to Jolene about them meeting up when they returned to England

and about how he would break it off with Jordan. They had planned their passionate meeting in the toilet and Jolene was heartbroken that Neil didn't appear to want her, now that he knew the real her. Penny seemed to be the only person who cared about her and was the only person to comfort her during her rejections.

Penny was getting fed up of feigning empathy. Jolene had gulped back tears for the last twenty minutes and Penny was looking forward to washing the tears that had been splattered onto her Chanel blouse away. 'Rancid' she thought, while gritting her teeth and wishing she had invested in another bottle of hand sanitiser. She knew Neil wouldn't show his weaselly face tonight and found the only motivation in watching him eat with his rotund girlfriend, was that it was keeping her on track with her diet. Penny looked at the menu, happy that she didn't have to watch the disgusting hordes cram chips on their plates. It hadn't appeared to stop the sounds of indecent loud chewing and echoing around her however. Penny decided on the Greek salad, believing it was the least disgusting option on the menu and her dinner companion chose the fish. "I am a vegetarian" said Jolene. Penny, fed up with being nice, said "I didn't think you disliked meat, especially sausage, after your recent antics." Jolene looked at her, aghast and not quite sure how to respond. "Well, meat is full of calories and fat, so I agree it is best you avoid it" said Penny, starting to relax and enjoying her little digs. She had always been told that she had a reputation for saying it how it is. Unfortunately Penny also had an entirely different reputation, which had always made her popular with males - if only for a five minute knee trembler. The thought of Neil exposing this spurred her into forcing some extra sympathy for Jolene who, much to Penny's disgust, chewed her fish noisily and gobbled rather than taking ladylike mouthfuls. Penny laid out the plan, explaining that she would find a really nosey old bat to tell the girlfriend that Neil had gone into the toilets with Jolene for sex She told Jolene that she should watch from a distance as the drama unfolded. This was mostly because Penny wanted to enjoy the drama alone and not be interrupted by the snivelling, chewing mess sitting with her.

Frank watched as the waiter passed his table, balancing two dishes of taramasalata expertly and presented them to Daddy and Zophia. "Look, its pink, that tarantula" said Agnes, nudging Frank in his ribs and causing him to wince. He wished she wouldn't do that. Daddy caught sight of Frank and Agnes looking across at his table. "Ah comrade, I recommend the taramasalata - it's divine!" Frank piped up in reply. "I'm not sure about eating spiders." Daddy laughed, as did the surrounding guests. "It's fish eggs, old boy!" Agnes went very pale. "Oooooh that's worse, we like English grub." Daddy nodded at her response. "Me too, but when in Rome, or in this case Greece..!" Daddy belly laughed at his own joke and Zophia smiled, although she looked as if she didn't really understand what was funny. Frank turned to the watching diners. "I knew it wasn't spider, it were a joke!" The diners looked unconvinced, as Frank and Agnes had Greek fish and potatoes put in front of them. Frank speared the fish with his fork. "There's no bloody batter on this fish, and where are the chips?" Agnes took a big mouthful of fish, as she was so hungry. "Ooooh it's not too bad, Frank. The potatoes are like little roast potatoes." Frank and Agnes gobbled down their food, asking for extra Greek potatoes. The restaurant finished serving and all the guests seemed happy, Agnes had decided she liked the baklava, after she had been convinced it wasn't the mask that armed robbers wore.

Ray and Jen sat at their table, discussing how nice the hotel was and how lucky they had been with the weather. Jen had popped into the local salon earlier and had her blond locks trimmed and blow dried. Ray had spent the day catching up on the horse and dog racing from home in an English owned bar in town and had drunk a fair few beer. Ray ordered the moussaka with Jen, after she had explained three times it was a type of lasagne, Greek style. The food arrived and Ray, who was already two sheets to the wind, decided to get up to go to the toilets. He stood up, wobbling alarmingly and dropped his napkin. He turned to pick it up but lost his balance and stumbled backwards, ending up sat in his Moussaka. The diners watched on in amusement as Ray staggered off to the gents, mince and cheese stuck to the back of his trousers. A waiter tried to follow to wipe it off, causing Ray to speed up and push his hand away, with a look of disgust. Jen laughed so hard her stomach hurt. A few minutes later Ray returned. "Did you see that waiter, Jen?" Jen stifled a giggle. "Yes Ray, you sat in your moussaka and he was trying to wipe the mince off your bum!" Ray looked alarmed. "He gave a mince, oh Jen!" at this point Jen was unable to hold her hysteria anymore. Once she explained in a way that Ray understood, they both laughed, although she noticed Ray spent the rest of the evening avoiding the waiter and either sitting down or standing with his back to the wall.

Stavros pulled on his traditional Greek dancing outfit regretting eating a gyros at lunchtime, as the white tights felt like they had shrunk around his hairy thighs. He also noticed the skirt had an unsightly stain at the back. He knew he shouldn't have sat on the old woman's lap the previous night at the Grove hotel - how was he supposed to know she had a colostomy bag? His dancing partner, Helen, waited for him in her traditional headscarf and dress, rolling her eyes and hoping the night would pass quickly. The Greek music started and both jumped into the restaurant, dancing frantically. Unfortunately old Mr Tarry, who was an elderly resident at the hotel and the spitting image of Robert de Niro, was so shocked by their entrance that he spluttered his sherry all over the table and clutched at his chest. "Bloody hell, you scared the shit out of me, you stupid sods!" Anna went to his table, calmly cleaned up the spilt sherry and attempted to calm down old Mr Tarry, who was still calling the dancers "Arseholes!" The music stopped after the first dance and Stavros addressed Mr Tarry with "Ya talkin ta me?" Mr Tarry looked straight back at Stavros, unblinkingly. "You want to make something of it, you stupid bastard?" Stavros withered under the stare of 'Tarry de Niro' and the room fell silent. Stavros felt his buttocks begin to twitch as Mr Tarry stood up, raising his fists. Luckily for Stavros, Mrs May was watching from the side of the restaurant and escorted Mr Tarry out of the room before he launched a full haymaker on Stavros.

Stavros and Helen burst into dance again to the amazement of Frank, who nudged Agnes. "Fellas wearing a skirt n' tights. See these foreigners, always a bit light on their toes." Agnes sat with a dirty grin on her face as she watched Stavros' skirt rise, revealing a tightly packed gusset. The guests cheered as the dance finished and Stavros then began walking around the tables, pulling scared looking women up to dance. He got to Agnes who jumped up enthusiastically, grabbing his hand. "Come on love, I love a good dance!" Stavros tried not to yelp as she held his hand in a vice-like grip. He quickly led her to Helen and the other woman, who were standing in a circle, and shoved her into the ring. Stavros got the guests shouting "OOOMPAH!" Agnes hitched up her skirt, revealing her hairy legs and started doing an impromptu dance of her own shouting "Ooompah, oompah, stick it up your jumper!" The crowds gathered to watch Agnes, swirling around in a dancing frenzy. Daddy leaned across to Zophia, clearing his throat." Now that's what happens when a woman gets too many ideas about burning bras and drinking men's drinks. They can't cope and go loopy. They even think they can cope without a man's guidance!" Zophia nodded to Daddy. "I think she talk politics earlier. She say about two people acting in loo cabinet earlier." Daddy sternly cleared his throat. "Women don't discuss politics, that's just the way it is. Don't worry your pretty little head about it." He patted her hand and reminded her of their lovely stately home, waiting for her woman's touch when they arrived back in England and how she could do lots of lovely flower arranging and soirees very soon.

Frank sat at his seat whooping and applauding Agnes, who currently had Stavros on her shoulder and was spinning him around so fast he was screaming, his face white with fear. The faster she spun, the more the vomit rose in his throat until the spinning finally caused it to spray from his mouth. Agnes threw him to the floor, where Stavros started to crawl away. Penny was already annoyed by the loud and common entertainment and had told Stavros if he tried to grab her hand again, she would break his hand. "I have had enough of this farce for tonight!" she screeched, throwing her chair back and rising to her feet. She then stormed out of the dining room followed by predator, who was wiping vomit out of her own hair. Zophia was crying inside as she used a napkin to clean her vomit stained dress. Daddy had used her a human shield against the Jetstream of rancid puke that had emitted from Stavros's mouth, as he was spun like a demented Catherine wheel. The guests were astounded as Daddy told her to "Pop up and shower old girl, that's the ticket. Must keep up appearances." Zophia trudged out of the restaurant, along with the other vomit laden guests.

Jessica and Justin watched the entertainment with awe and repulsion from the security office - the new CCTV was working a treat. Jessica was fretting about the table linen and was deeply troubled by the whole incident, repeating how ghastly the whole event was. Justin could only laugh. The more he laughed, the more Jessica seemed to relax. With one final glance at each other, they burst out laughing again, until their bellies hurt. Wiping his eyes and still giggling, Justin spoke of how he wished Penny had been in the vomit line of fire. "It's about time that poisonous trout got what's coming to her." Jessica hugged Justin and promised "I will get her to leave, she can't stay here forever on my money." Justin had thought long and hard about moving to Greece over the last few days. He knew Jessica had warmed to owning the hotel and decided to ask her outright. "Jessica, how would you feel about us living here permanently?" Jessica smiled in response. "I would love that!" They both walked hand in hand to their apartment, making future.

CHAPTER 16

Neil woke up next to Jordan, the sunlight shining through the window. They had shared their last evening on holiday eating McDonalds on the beach and drinking in the local bars. Neil had worked hard not stare at any other women, which had been torture as there were numerous attractive women running around in next to nothing in the evening heat. Jordan had enjoyed herself; he knew. He had made sure of it. He also knew he had to save his reputation and he didn't want to end up homeless. Neil went to the restaurant, so he could take breakfast back to the room for them both. He didn't want Jordan to bump into predator or Penny, as he knew they would have been scheming. He had seen them together, whispering and it had caused the hairs on his grubby neck to rise. He knew that Penny would never want her identity exposed and he was willing to blackmail her with that information to get out of this murky situation.

He walked into the restaurant, noticing quickly that all eyes were on him. 'They can't know about what happened with predator' he thought. While waiting for his order, he noticed Penny in the lounge and tried to hide, but it was too late - she sauntered over. "Look Pen, if you cause any trouble with Jordan, I will expose you." Penny turned to Neil "Oh, but my featherweight boxer friend, I know all about your antics in the toilet. I will expose you!" Neil staggered back in disbelief. "Oh yes, I know everything about your liaison in the toilets, Jolene has spread the love, shall we say? I would make an appointment with your GP when you return home!!" Neil clenched his fists in anger. "I will expose you "he repeated. Penny laughed loudly. "I will expose myself, if need be." Neil sniggered. "See, same old Pen. Clothes off and legs akimbo!" Penny giggled in reply. "Not for you though, ratty. Have a safe journey home, ta ta!" She walked off, leaving Neil to curse loudly. He scurried off and collected the breakfasts – he'd already been downstairs too long. Jordan waited in the room for Neil to return, feeling happy for the first time in a long time. Finally, he returned, and they ate their breakfasts on the balcony. "Neil, our coach is not until this afternoon. Shall we sunbathe and have a few drinks by the bar?" she suggested. Neil sat bolt upright in his chair in panic. "Don't you want to stay in here, keep out the sun?" Jordan shook her head and insisted that she wanted to sit by the bar with a nice cold pint, enjoying their last day in the sun. There was nothing Neil could do, apart from pray that he got through the next few hours without his girlfriend finding out the awful truth of what had happened in the toilets.

Neil walked with Jordan to the bar like a condemned man, his feet feeling like they were made of lead. They walked past the pool to the bar, with all eyes on them. "Why they all are looking at us, Neil?" Neil thought quickly. "Because you look gorgeous." Jordan smiled and replied "Awwwww Neil, I do love you." Neil started sweating from more than just the heat as he ordered drinks at the bar. He could see all the guests were watching their every move. This was worse than he had expected, it appeared that the whole of the hotel knew his dirty secret!

Ray picked his newly tailored trousers up from reception. He was going to go and try them on straight away, now that the waist would be four inches smaller, he hoped they would fit perfectly. Penny looked around the restaurant and found the perfect start to her plan in the gossip merchant of Agnes. She sat on the next table to Agnes and Frank and smiled warmly. Agnes nudged Frank. "Why is that stuck up cow smiling at me?" and gave Penny a fixed grin back. She approached the table. "Hello Agnes. Frank. Apologies we got off on the wrong foot, but I need advice and clearly you are the only sensible people who can help." Agnes leaned forward on the table, to look closer at Penny's face. "How can we help, love?" Penny tried to keep her smirk hidden. "Well, have you seen that horrible rat face boy? The one who is meant to be here with his lovely girlfriend?" Agnes bristled. "The one that ad it away with that old tart in the toilets, you mean? Dirty beggar." Penny felt elated that this was going to plan so quickly. "I just feel sorry for that poor girlfriend because she doesn't know and to be honest, the whole hotel knows and are laughing about it. I just don't know what to do." Agnes sat bolt upright. "Someone needs to tell her, poor cow, it's only right. Let me go have a shower and I will find the poor girl and tell 'er." Penny smiled sweetly at Agnes. "I just knew you would know the right thing to do." Agnes preened at Penny's compliments. "Give me 'alf an hour, see ya by the pool love." Agnes walked off with a purposeful stride, her husband Frank limping behind her.

'Perfect' thought Penny, as she spotted Zophia in the lounge. "Hello, you look like a woman who will understand my situation." Zophia looked at Penny. "Hello darling, I am waiting for my husband's English newspaper, he must have it. How can I help you?" Penny explained how Jordan had been cheated on by Neil in the toilets. Zophia flared her nostrils. "Filthy ratman pig! I would string him up and torture him with big knife. I will tell the pig he is disgusting. Now where is this English paper?" Penny walked to the pool and took up a nice position to wait for the fun to begin. She was happy to see that Neil and Jordan were sitting in the pool bar. She sidled closer to the bar to listen in when Agnes appeared with Frank and, as if timed to perfection, Zophia arrived in the bar with Daddy. She saw Neil look around furtively, presumably checking that predator was not around. Penny had taken care of that problem. Predator was watching from the side of the pool, completely dressed and wearing a baseball hat and large sunglasses. Neil went off to the toilets and Penny watched as Agnes approached Jordan. She saw the look of horror on Jordan's face as Agnes bellowed out what a rat Neil was. Jordan instantly ordered alcohol and started drinking shot after shot.

Jordan felt rage building up in her. That nice old lady had told her what Neil had done with that ageing old tart. And everyone knew except her! He'd done the business with the sagging harlot in a dirty toilet, then slept with her and promised her the world! No wonder he had been nice to her in the last 24 hours. She felt a complete fool. Then she saw him strutting back towards the bar. "HOW ABOUT YOU GET EMBARRASSED FOR A CHANGE!" she screamed, throwing his beer at him "YOU DIRTY CHEATING, UGLY RAT! YOU CAN PACK YOUR BAGS WHEN YOU WE GET HOME AND SOD OFF!" The guests all starting cheering. Zophia stood up too "Yes you rat, I can't believe you did that in those disgusting toilets!" Daddy looked at Zophia in horror. Jordan jumped up and continued shouting "YOU ARE A RAT FACED, SKINNY RUNT AND YOU WERE NEVER A BLOODY BOXER" she yelled, her fist connecting with his jaw. Neil flew backwards, seemingly in slow motion, his sunglasses hurtling to the side as landed hard against the barstools, right on his bony backside. He lay motionless as the guests whooped and cheered.

Anna went over to check on Neil. "He just sleeping" she said and stepped over him. Daddy turned to Zophia. "I say, no need to get carried away. Women just don't act like that!" Jordan turned to him, her face still full of rage. "If you don't shut up, I will give you a knuckle supper too!" Daddy cleared his throat. "I am flabbergasted! Who do you think you are, threatening a man with violence? This really is the bally limit! Zophia, get me a brandy. Come on, quick sticks" Jordan downed another shot of vodka. "Where is the tramp he cheated on me with?" Penny seized her moment and sidled up to the bar, sitting next to a re faced and fists clenched Jordan. "I hate to tell you this, but that awful woman also has an STI. Lumps down below, I believe." Jordan stood up, the barstool falling behind her. "What?!" she screeched. She then vowed to ruin Neil's life, goaded on by Penny, who was enjoying every second.

Jordan felt humiliated and berated herself for not knowing Neil was up to something! For years she had put up with his snide remarks, his cheating and his laziness. She knew everyone was looking at her and was either laughing at her, or feeling sorry for her. She now had the extra concern that the dirty, vile moron had passed on an STI to her. She dearly wished that she had seen Neil for the disgusting scumbag he was years ago. She felt too angry to cry and had felt great satisfaction when her fist had connected with his jaw and watching him fly backwards with that shocked expression on his face. She downed another pint. The old posh man kept annoying her by tutting at her behaviour, so she turned on him again, threatening to stuff his stupid hat right up his bum, before launching herself at him. Luckily, Agnes jumped in and pulled her back. Zophia sat back, watching the entertainment and dearly wishing that the awful hat had been stuck up right up Daddy's big, old, wrinkly arse. While the commotion was going on, Officer Carras entered the bar and saw Neil on the floor. Anna explained in Greek what had happened, and the policeman tried hard not to laugh. Nothing shocked him anymore, especially where the English were concerned. He sat and ordered a pint of beer, sad that he had missed the entertainment.

Neil felt very woozy when he came around, his head hurt, and he felt a raging pain in his jaw. He then saw Jordan arguing with the posh old git at the bar and being restrained by that big woman, who was married to the limping war hero. Neil tried to crawl away, only to be stopped by Penny, who was looking down at him with a menacing grin. "Don't ever mess with me" she said, in a threatening voice and walked off to join the other parties arguing in the bar. Neil continued to crawl away in the direction of the reception lounge and as he looked across the room, he saw redator, blowing him a kiss. 'Bitch' he thought. He continued to crawl across and finally pulled his skinny body over the reception threshold and onto the leather sofa. He knew the coach would be arriving soon to take them all to the airport and his case was already in reception. He just had to ensure that the holiday rep would protect him on the journey to the plane. He fell into a deep sleep and awoke to a full reception area crowded with guests, all waiting to catch their coach to the airport. He looked frantically around for somewhere to hide as he heard Jordon shout, "There he is, there's the bastard!" and directed the holiday rep towards Neil.

The room fell silent as predator entered the reception and Jordan spotted her straight away. "You dirty old slag! You can't have been that good because he came back to me to finish off!" Predator laughed and retaliated quickly "Well I am more woman than you, fatso!" Jordan flew forward, only to be held back by Mrs May, in order to allow the Holiday rep to try and calm the situation. Mummy watched the events unfold, trying desperately to clamp her hand over Mounir's ears. "I don't want you hearing naughty words" she hissed, as her son struggled to watch the commotion, cheering Jordan on. Ahmed also seemed caught up in the moment, jumping up and down and shouting "Bastard!" He wasn't quite sure who he was shouting about, but the atmosphere was electric. Mummy gave Ahmed a scathing look. "Don't join in with the riff-raff!" Ahmed seemed to calm a little after that. Ray entered the reception right in the middle of the commotion, wearing very short, cropped trousers. "You took four inches off the leg, not the waist!" he shouted. The whole crowd turned to look at him and Jen pointed at a man wearing shorts. "Oh, look Ray, he has the same tailor as you!" Ray saw the funny side and started laughing with Jen, who quickly tried to fill him in as to the commotion happening around them. She repeated it three times to Ray, who kept talking about his trousers and laughing.

Daddy had been stewing over the events in the bar. He was disgusted by the whole affair but something else that had been niggling at him finally came to light. He suddenly remembered Frank Small! And in a fit of anger Daddy marched into the reception, shouting "FRANK SMALL! I REMEMBER YOU! YOU NEVER MADE IT TO THE WAR, YOU FELL DOWN A POTHOLE!" Daddy remembered the whole incident as, when on the morning of setting off for Vietnam, word had got to him that he would be a man down due to some silly sod falling down a pothole and refusing to fight! Daddy shouted at Frank, calling him a cad and a bounder and he told him he deserved to be given a white feather! The guests all stared at Frank, who walked out of the hotel to the coach very much without a limp, muttering to Agnes. "I hope the social don't hear about this" and put his head down, while his wife held hers up high.

Neil then decided to join in with all the exposes and piped up. "Penny, you are Penny Smith and a prostitute." The room once again looked on, waiting for the next bit of gossip. Penny froze, all eyes on her and try to laugh. "I am a respectable married woman, aren't I Jessica?" Jessica looked at Penny, finally realising what a horrid old snob she was. "Are you, Penny? Either way, I would like you to leave my hotel. Now." Penny had never expected Jessica to speak to her like that. She panicked and looked across to Jolene, who jumped to her new friend's aid. "Come on Penny, you don't need these imbeciles!" Penny stormed up to Jessica and whispered in her ear "Actually, I am a high-class hooker, darling. Far too good for you and this shithole of a hotel!" Jessica seized her chance to rid herself of Penny once and for all. "Just leave!" Penny looked startled. "Go on!" screamed Jessica. "Piss off, you disgusting munter!" The remaining guests stared at Penny, as she stormed towards the exit, shouting at Jessica "You will regret this!"

Jessica and Justin watched as the coach left the hotel and gave a huge sigh of relief. "Surely the next guests won't be as bad..." said Jessica, as another coach pulled up outside.

Three star with a touch of Caviar

ABOUT THE AUTHOR

Caroline Briault is a new author with Three star and a touch of Caviar being the first book in a series she has created. She became inspired to write after a hilarious holiday to Greece. Not currently s full time writer but Caroline hopes this may be something she can become in the future. Mrs. Briault lives with her husband in a quiet down in East Sussex with her lovable Rottweiler Dexter. You can visit her online at https://www.facebook.com/groups/500961627233171/?ref=gs &fref=gs&dti=500961627233171&hc_location=group

Printed in Great Britain
by Amazon

37131057R00097